Associate Professor Akira Takatsuki's Conjecture

1

Folklore Studies

Mikage Sawamura

YEN
ON

NEW YORK

Associate Professor
Akira Takatsuki's Conjecture

Mikage Sawamura
Translation by Katelyn Smith

JUNKYOJU · TAKATSUKIAKIRA NO SUISATSU Vol. 1 MINZOKUGAKU KAKU KATARIKI
©Mikage Sawamura 2018
First published in Japan in 2018 by KADOKAWA CORPORATION, Tokyo.
English translation rights arranged with KADOKAWA CORPORATION, Tokyo, through Tuttle-Mori Agency, Inc., Tokyo.

English translation © 2023 by Yen Press, LLC

Yen On
150 West 30th Street, 19th Floor
New York, NY 10001

Visit us at yenpress.com ✴ facebook.com/yenpress ✴ twitter.com/yenpress
yenpress.tumblr.com ✴ instagram.com/yenpress

First Yen On Edition: May 2023
Edited by Yen On Editorial: Payton Campbell
Designed by Yen Press Design: Madelaine Norman

Yen On is an imprint of Yen Press, LLC.
The Yen On name and logo are trademarks of Yen Press, LLC.

Library of Congress Cataloging-in-Publication Data
Names: Sawamura, Mikage, author. | Smith, Katelyn, translator.
Title: Associate professor Akira Takatsuki's conjecture / Mikage Sawamura ; translated by Katelyn Smith.
Other titles: Junkyouju Takatsuki Akira no suisatsu. English
Description: First Yen On edition. | New York, NY : Yen On, 2023- | Contents: v. 1. Folklore studies —
Identifiers: LCCN 2022058928 | ISBN 9781975352974 (v. 1 ; trade paperback) | ISBN 9781975352998 (v. 2 ; trade paperback) | ISBN 9781975353018 (v. 3 ; trade paperback) | ISBN 9781975353032 (v. 4 ; trade paperback) | ISBN 9781975353056 (v. 5 ; trade paperback) | ISBN 9781975353070 (v. 6 ; trade paperback) | ISBN 9781975353094 (v. 7 ; trade paperback)
Subjects: CYAC: Ability—Fiction. | Teacher-student relationships—Fiction. | LCGFT: Light novels.
Classification: LCC PZ7.1.S284 As 2023 | DDC [Fic]—dc23
LC record available at https://lccn.loc.gov/2022058928

ISBNs: 978-1-9753-5297-4 (paperback)
       978-1-9753-5298-1 (ebook)

10 9 8 7 6 5 4 3 2 1

LSC-C

Printed in the United States of America

Contents

It happened one summer night when I was ten years old.
I was visiting my grandmother's house in Nagano.

Her house was in a mountain village far from the train station. My family visited every year during the summer and winter holidays. My other relatives would visit around the same time, and I really enjoyed playing with my cousins, who I rarely got to see.
But that year, I caught a terrible summer cold.
Despite already feeling a bit ill, I rather unwisely played in a stream with my cousins and got soaking wet. I came down with a high fever that lasted for days, and I couldn't even get out of bed.
When the day of the festival—which was held at the local shrine—arrived, my fever still hadn't subsided.
I had been looking forward to that festival more than anything. The shrine itself was on top of the mountain and could only be reached by climbing a long, long flight of stairs, but the festival was held at the mountain's base. In the square beneath the mountain, under the bright-red glow of the countless round, red paper lanterns hung among the many vendors' stalls, everyone would join in the festival dance around the tall wooden stage. I had been saving up for that day for weeks.
I was going to go to the festival. I had to. But no matter how many times I insisted, no one let me go. Frustrated and sad, I cried into my futon, and when one of my cousins finally came home from the festival and hesitantly presented me with a *Super Sentai* mask, saying, "Here's a souvenir. One of the stalls was selling them," I cried again. Before I knew it, I had cried myself to sleep.

I was awoken by the thundering boom of festival drums.

I got up in a hurry, expecting to be dizzy with fever, but found I felt totally fine. I thought if I was feeling better, it would be okay to go out.

Something seemed off, however.

The house was pitch-black, and everyone appeared to be asleep.

A glance at the clock revealed it was past midnight. There was no way the festival would still be going on at that hour.

But I could clearly hear the thundering of the drums.

Boom, boom, buh-boom. That echoing sound was unmistakable. It was the sound of the large drum being beaten on top of the stage. The festival was definitely still happening. Once I realized that, I couldn't help myself.

Still in my nightclothes, I crept quietly out of my grandmother's house.

In my naive young mind, the *Sentai* mask at my bedside would act as a disguise, so I put it on as I departed. I would definitely have been scolded for going outside that late if I had been discovered.

I ran as fast as I could down the road in the dead of night toward the sound of the drums.

When I arrived at the festival site, there were people everywhere.

Adults, children. People in light summer *yukata* and heavier kimonos, people in Western clothes. The crowd that surrounded the wooden stage was two to three people deep, and they were all dancing. The festival wasn't over, after all.

I noted with disappointment that the stalls had all closed up already, but I was happy enough just to be able to join in the dancing for a little while. Bravely adjusting the mask on my face, I stepped into the square.

But something felt wrong.

The lanterns—the paper lanterns hung around the festival site were blue.

All of them. Festival lanterns were always red—everyone knew that, and yet... The innumerable strings of blue lanterns looked just like will-o'-the-wisps floating in the night. They emitted a pale, cold light. I had never seen paper lanterns like this before.

And why couldn't I hear anything except the thundering of the drums?

It was a festival. Normally, the festival music would be blaring loudly from the speakers installed in the square. But that night, the speakers were silent. Two adults stood atop the wooden stage, devotedly beating the drums, and that was all. *Boom, boom, buh-boom.*

There was something else—something even stranger.

I could not hear even a single voice...

...despite being among that many people.

I looked closely and saw that everyone, adults and children alike, was wearing a mask. Fire-breathing jester masks, round-faced woman masks, masks that resembled the face of an old man. They all danced in sync around the stage, silently swaying to the thundering of the drums. *Boom, boom, buh-boom.* I looked up at the only source of sound—the resounding thundering of the drums that shook the stage down to its base.

The blue will-o'-the-wisp lanterns. The masked people silently circling the stage.

It was all so terribly unreal—like a scene from another world.

Maybe I was dreaming.

That thought drifted dimly into my mind when it happened.

Suddenly, someone grabbed my shoulder.

I whirled around in surprise to see a man in a fire-breathing jester mask.

"...What are you doing here?"

The man spoke in a hushed voice that filled me with confusion.

That voice was familiar. It sounded like my grandfather.

Why would my grandfather be there?

"Why did you come here? You shouldn't be here... Hey, don't take off your mask. No matter what."

I had started to remove my mask to get a better look at who I was talking to, but he stopped me.

My grandfather crouched and looked into my eyes through the holes in his mask.

He said, "Get out of here right now. Don't let anyone see—"

My grandfather suddenly turned to look over his shoulder at the other people.

Some of the swaying, trembling dancers were looking at us.

Round-faced woman masks, old lady masks, cat masks. With their arms swaying and feet stomping to the thundering of the drums, they had craned their necks to an unnatural degree to stare right at my grandfather and me.

"It's too late. They noticed you," my grandfather said.

What did he mean by *too late*? Who in the world were the dancing people?

I had so many questions, but for some reason I was too afraid to voice them.

"...You have to pay the price. Come on."

My grandfather's hand clamped onto my arm with an iron grip. He led me like that to the corner of the square.

I thought perhaps he would let me escape at that point, but I was wrong.

There was a single stall in the spot I was taken to.

I had thought all the stalls were closed, but that one alone seemed to be open. A man stood inside, wearing a black demon mask and a traditional coat, not saying a word.

Behind the stall, the mountain with the shrine at its peak rose up. Its looming shadow spread down from the sky, and it felt like it was staring at me. Looking up, I saw that the blue lanterns had also been hung along the stairs leading to the shrine. Blue dots of light shone here and there all the way to the top of the mountain. It looked like a path meant to welcome something that wasn't human.

My grandfather whispered into my ear.

"Choose just one. You don't need to pay."

On top of the stall's counter were sweets, the kind usually sold at festivals. A candied apple, a candied plum, and an amber-colored lollipop. Only one of each.

My grandfather pointed at the apple.

"If you choose that one, you won't be able to walk."

After he told me that, I couldn't help but view the red apple sitting in front of me as though it were poisoned.

My grandfather pointed at the candied plum.

"If you choose that one, you'll lose your words."

What did that mean? Would it burn my throat? Would I lose my tongue? Whatever the case, I was petrified beyond words.

Finally, my grandfather pointed at the lollipop.

"If you choose that one, you—"

What? What could it be? What horrible thing would happen to me? My grandfather spoke into my ear as I stood, stiff.

"You will—"

When I heard the answer, I thought, *That's much better than the other two options.*

At the time, I didn't truly understand the meaning of the words he'd uttered. They were words I had read in books, but I didn't know what they meant in reality.

Therefore, without hesitation, I chose the amber lollipop.

I was instructed to eat it then and there, and I obediently followed suit.

I will never forget the sweet flavor that melted over my tongue.

By chance...

If I were able to return to that night...

I wonder, if I were faced with that same choice, which one would I pick?

No matter how often I try, I can't come up with an answer.

But I cannot help but think that I made the wrong choice that night.

Chapter 1:
The Neighbor Who Shouldn't Exist

If asked why he decided to head into the first lecture for Folklore Studies II that day, Naoya Fukamachi would have said, "Just because."

Earlier that spring, Naoya had become a first-year student of the Literature Department at Seiwa University.

A private university located in Tokyo's Chiyoda City, the home page of Seiwa's website claimed that respecting the freedom and individuality of its students was part of the school's academic culture.

In Naoya's opinion, students' freedom and individuality were totally respected more at the university level in general, at least as compared to high school.

To begin with, students could choose for themselves which courses to take. Aside from the compulsory subjects, they could take any general education classes they liked to meet credit requirements. Looking at the registration information and course outlines he had been handed along with a blank timetable, Naoya was keenly aware of how different high school was from college.

On the other hand, being able to make his own schedule also meant he had no one to blame but himself if he ended up signing up for a course that didn't agree with him. Naoya wanted to avoid taking classes that were boring or too difficult, if possible, but it was hard to make a judgment based on the course outline alone. If he wanted to know whether a class he was unsure of was worth taking, he had no choice but to attend the first lecture.

Folklore Studies II was one of the Literature Department's general education courses.

Naoya wasn't particularly interested in folklore. Or rather, he wasn't quite sure what kind of knowledge comprised folklore studies in the first place. For some reason, he imagined it involved researching regional festivals and folktales.

But the explanatory summary written for the course's outline was a little interesting.

It said: "From school ghost stories to urban legends and so on, we will take a broad approach to the field of folklore studies."

"School ghost stories and urban legends." The course contents sounded just like an episode of a TV variety show, and Naoya was curious about whether such subjects were really going to be the theme of the class.

The class met on Wednesdays during third period. School building 1, classroom 201.

The professor was Akira Takatsuki—an associate professor of historical literature specializing in folklore and antiquities.

When he entered the classroom, Naoya was surprised to see that most of the seats were already filled, even though the room was a large, tiered lecture hall. He didn't think folklore studies were particularly in demand, but the course seemed quite popular.

Inside the classroom, the energy and noise of the other students filled the air. Naoya frowned reflexively. He had struggled with being in crowded places since he was younger.

For a moment, he thought about leaving but changed his mind after considering that he might as well stay after making the effort to find the class. He didn't want to waste his time by turning and walking away without even hearing the lecture. Naoya stuffed his earbuds in both ears, pressed PLAY on his MP3 player, and pushed up the bridge of his glasses. Then he steeled his resolve and started down the tiered aisle toward the remaining empty seats in the front of the class.

As he went, he met the eyes of a brown-haired male student. The other student's name escaped him, but Naoya was fairly sure they had been in the same required linguistics course.

Noticing Naoya in return, he said "Hey" and raised one hand slightly. "You're taking this class, too?"

"Ah, yeah, I think so."

Naoya paused his music and took just one earbud out to reply.

"Yeah, I think I probably will, too. It seems like the guy who teaches it, Takatsuki, is some kind of celebrity. This guy isn't even in our department, but he came all the way here just to hear the lecture."

Brown Hair pointed to the student sitting next to him, who appeared to be his friend, while he spoke.

Students in any department could take general education classes for credit. It seemed like the classroom was so full because the attendees were from a mix of other departments.

But still, what did Brown Hair mean by *celebrity*? Had the professor been on television or something?

"Oh yeah," Brown Hair said, leaning forward a bit just as Naoya was going to ask about Professor Takatsuki's evident fame.

"Listen, a group of us from English class are going out drinking tonight. You coming?"

"...What? Isn't it a bit soon to be going out drinking together?"

Naoya instinctively forced a smile at the invitation.

College students had a reputation for doing nothing but going out to drink. Maybe that was accurate. Most of the first-year students were likely still minors, though.

"It's better to get to know each other early, isn't it? Plus, we can share info about lectures and student clubs with each other. So you gonna join us? There will be girls there, too."

"Ah... Sorry, I can't tonight."

Naoya gave his ambiguous excuse, and Brown Hair accepted it read-ily with a nod.

"Well, I'm sure we'll do it again. Next time, you should come."

"Yeah, thanks. Well."

Naoya waved good-bye a little, then started heading down the steps again.

He could hear Brown Hair and his friend talking behind him.

"Who was that plain-looking four-eyes? Friend of yours?"

"Oh, we're in linguistics together. We all had to introduce ourselves in English, and he was sitting close to me, so I remembered him from that... I forget his name, though..."

"So you can't really say you remember him, then."

They were even, it seemed, as far as forgetting each other's names.

Listening to the two talking behind him, Naoya thought perhaps it was his fault for being a plain-looking four-eyes.

It was typical for people to take the opportunity to completely change their outer appearances and become fashionable upon entering college, but Naoya had no desire to be part of that crowd. In any case, since he had started living alone in the spring, his financial situation had been difficult. What was wrong with wearing the same hoodie and jeans he had been sporting since high school?

Besides, plain was exactly what he was aiming for—he didn't want to stand out.

Finally reaching an empty seat two rows from the front, Naoya sat down.

Then, from the row directly behind him, he overheard two girls having a conversation. One of the girls had a clear voice, and the other spoke with a slight lisp, her tone saccharine.

"Speaking of, Yuki, did you decide which club to join?"

"Huh? Not yet. But I thought maybe I should play tennis."

"You played tennis in high school, too, right? I'm interested in the broadcasting society."

"Ooh, that's a good idea. Kana, you're great at speaking, so I bet you'd be good at making announcements and stuff. Oh, so anyway, about the mixer I mentioned yesterday—"

"Ah, sorry. **I have plans** on Friday."

Suddenly, the clear voice of the first girl wobbled and *warped*.

It was as if someone was using a machine to randomly alter the pitch of her voice. It oscillated between a deep, sonorous tone that was nothing like her original one and a metallic, high-pitched creak.

Naoya looked over his shoulder while fighting off the chills crawling up his spine.

One short-haired girl, one with long, fluffy hair. The two of them carried on talking as if nothing had happened.

"Really? Well, if you're busy, there's nothing we can do about it."

"Yeah, sorry. I'll make it up to you soon."

"It's fine, I'll just try talking to the other girls. But you'll come to the next one, right, Kana?"

"Yeah, of course, **I'll definitely go next time.**"

As her voice distorted again, the short-haired girl cast a questioning glance in Naoya's direction. Flustered, Naoya turned back around in his seat.

As he did, he called out quietly in his mind to the long-haired girl.

I don't think the girl sitting next to you likes mixers.

All at once, the hustle and bustle of the classroom began to ring in Naoya's ears. People talking to those around them, students speaking into their smartphones, conversations filling the air.

"No way, seriously? **I was on the basketball team through all of high school**, though."

"Whaaat? **I don't have** Rikako's contact info."

"Shut up, you guys! I'm telling you **it wasn't my mom calling; it was my girlfriend!**"

"It was a joke! Don't take it seriously! **That outfit looks great on you!**"

The warped, twisting voices came from all over the huge classroom, becoming an unbearable cacophony.

Naoya covered his ears and put his head down. Several bursts of laughter sounded from somewhere behind him. *I don't know how any of you can laugh with all this noise*, he thought. The long-haired girl sitting behind him spoke again, her voice loud and jarring like a broken violin. *It's too loud. It's too loud.* Naoya felt sick, like he was suffocating. This was why he couldn't stand being around so many people. He should have left class, after all.

Unable to tolerate the noise, he reached for his MP3 player, which was still on pause.

Then—

"Yes, hello."

—that voice.

There was no warping. Naoya heard it with surprising directness. It was like a single ray of white light shining through the muddy, stagnant air.

Instinctively, Naoya raised his head in the direction of that voice.

Unnoticed, a man had come to stand at the teaching podium.

The man was holding a microphone, so he had to be the associate professor teaching the course, but he looked quite young. His tall, slender form was dressed in a well-tailored three-piece suit.

"Huh?" the man muttered, looking down at the microphone.

"Ah, sorry. It wasn't turned on."

The man's voice started coming through the sound system. The noise in the lecture hall turned to laughter. Behind Naoya, the two girls he had overheard before were giggling as well.

"Omigod, what was that? So cute!"

"He's a total hottie, don't you think? I'm definitely gonna take this class!"

The girls whispered back and forth about the professor.

He was indeed handsome. He had large, half-lidded eyes and a straight nose. A warm, friendly smile sat on his thin lips. His features were clean-cut and had an air of gentleness about them—his face was truly worthy of the "sweet mask" label found so often in novels. His hair was tinged with brown, and it was difficult to tell whether it had been dyed or was naturally that shade.

"Allow me to properly introduce myself. I'm Takatsuki, the Folklore Studies II professor. Congratulations to all you new students on matriculating, and welcome back to the second- and third-years."

Then Akira Takatsuki surveyed the classroom with a slight nod.

His voice was crystal clear. Its tone was a bit high for a man, and it reached Naoya's ears gently even through the microphone. It seemed Takatsuki's appeal wasn't limited to his handsome face; he had a nice voice as well. Some people really were blessed.

But there was something Naoya couldn't quite put his finger on.

Why did the sound of that voice make him feel like he could breathe easier?

"Hey, can you believe this? Apparently, Professor Takatsuki's thirty-four!"

"What? No way! He looks like he's in his twenties! So he's already an associate professor at this age, and he's handsome, too? Ooh, is he single? Married? Does it say anywhere?"

It appeared the girls behind Naoya had immediately begun looking up the professor on their smartphones.

"Oh, look. Professor Takatsuki *has* been on TV before. He was on a paranormal television special commentating on spirits, and 'Who is this sexy associate professor?' became a trending topic on Twitter."

"Ah, I think I saw something about that."

I see, Naoya thought, listening to the conversation happening behind him. So that's what Brown Hair had meant earlier when he said Takatsuki was like a celebrity.

"Now then, can anyone here tell me what is involved in the field of folklore studies? Ah, you there with the smartphone. Sorry, but would you mind looking up the definition of *folklore studies* for us?"

Takatsuki was speaking to the girl sitting behind Naoya. She and her friend had been in full view of the lectern while they were talking and using their phones.

"Oh! Um...! It says... 'A f-field primarily focused on the study of the history of the development of common peoples' lives and culture as examined through the lens of folklore.'"

Despite her nerves from suddenly being called on, the girl with the long fluffy hair read out the result she had found online.

Takatsuki smiled.

"The digital *Daijisen* definition, right? Thank you. But as expected, the dictionary definition is a bit limited, isn't it? One might not automatically understand what 'through the lens of folklore' means here... *Folklore* refers to the customs, legends, folktales, proverbs, songs, dances, and so on that have been passed down through the generations. In general, customs are the things that we continue to do to this day, even if we don't really know why we're doing them, simply because people have been doing them for a long time. Things like scattering beans and eating uncut sushi rolls on the last day of winter, for example. These customs are repeated for years and years, and legends are handed down from parent to child. We folklorists study why such things started and how they have evolved through the years. The background behind the birth of an old folktale, the reason a festival came to be held. In this way, we can learn about the lives of groups of people and the state of their minds. That is folklore. Kunio Yanagita's folklore research and Shinobu Orikuchi's *marebito* theory are quite famous, so I'm sure some of you have read or heard about them somewhere."

Little by little, the students' murmuring was dying down.

Only Takatsuki's voice echoed throughout the quiet classroom.

"It's possible some of you may already have heard of me. 'I saw this guy on TV talking all snobbishly about spirits and such,' you might say. Indeed, I have made such appearances before. That's because my current research primarily has to do with mysterious circumstances and the supernatural. Scary stories, bizarre ones, spirits and apparitions—I'm particularly interested in modern-day ghost stories and urban legends.

Ones like Hanako-san, the girl who haunts school toilets, or the slit-mouthed woman, even if that one is a little antiquated. I study how such tales came to be told, as well as the stories that appear to be the source material for them."

In truth, Naoya had been wondering if such topics were actually academic. Was this good-looking guy really researching these things?

Nevertheless, the students in the lecture hall were, without a doubt, beginning to show interest in what Takatsuki was saying. No one was talking or looking at their smartphones anymore.

Naoya was starting to take an interest as well. He didn't really care about urban legends, but even so, Takatsuki's words were intriguing.

Above all, Takatsuki himself seemed the most enthralled, judging by his face. His eyes were glittering like a child's.

In the few days since he had started school, Naoya had attended several classes. He had experienced a variety of professors and lecturers, each with their own style of teaching. There were professors who read aloud from textbooks they themselves had authored, droning on and on without making eye contact with their students at all. Associate professors who went on listing technical terms without being bothered about their audience's level of comprehension. Instructors who proceeded matter-of-factly with their lecture while ignoring students who were playing on their phones or dozing off in the very first session. Compared to all those, this class was by far the most enjoyable.

"So I have two requests for you all. First, I would like you to help me with my research."

Takatsuki looked around the room again as he spoke.

"I have a website called Neighborhood Stories. There's a link to it on the Folklore Studies page of the Seiwa University site, so please check it out later. There are examples of urban legends I've heard so far and their classification on the site, but I'm also accepting submissions from the public. If you have any such stories, or have had any strange experiences, or know about any mysterious happenings at your own schools, I would love for you to post them... Ah, but please don't make up any stories or submit fake ones. While made-up folktales can be quite interesting because they become the basis for new urban legends, they get in the way during analysis and research. Erm, well, let me show you what I mean."

Takatsuki picked up the chalk for the first time and faced the blackboard.

He started scrawling on the board immediately, but he wasn't writing words. It looked like...some kind of...rotund serpent? *Yeah, that's a snake...probably*, thought Naoya. It was legless, had a thin tail, and the zigzagging line sticking out of its gaping mouth was most likely its tongue.

"This is Tsuchinoko."

Takatsuki pointed at the drawing as he made his declaration.

The room erupted into laughter. Clearly, artistic talent was not one of this man's many blessings.

"We will revisit Tsuchinoko in a future lecture, so there's no need to take notes today... As I'm sure many of you know, Tsuchinoko is a UMA—that's an *unidentified mysterious animal*—that was big in Japan during the 1970s. Its body is between one to three feet long—and thick and stubby. It has a triangular head and a slender tail. We can actually trace Tsuchinoko's origins back quite a ways. A plains deity called Nozuchi is mentioned in both of Japan's earliest chronicles: The *Kojiki* and the *Nihon shoki*. Nozuchi also appears in the *Wakan Sansai Zue*—an encyclopedia compiled during the Edo period—and it is believed that this deity is Tsuchinoko. There have been sightings all the way from Tohoku in the north down to Kyushu, and rewards of up to three hundred million yen offered for it, but to this day we still don't understand what Tsuchinoko is."

Next to his drawing, Takatsuki wrote *Historic chronicles: Nozuchi (plains deity)* and *Wakan Sansai Zue: Nozuchi serpent* in smooth script. Compared to the clumsiness of the picture, his handwriting was quite tidy.

"Now, let's say someone submits a report to my website saying they saw Tsuchinoko in Yokohama."

Takatsuki rapped on the Tsuchinoko drawing with his knuckles.

"First, I would be overjoyed."

The room broke into laughter again.

"Next, I would try to corroborate the report. I would meet with the person who submitted the report if possible and have them show me around the area where the sighting took place. Then I would spend some time hunting for Tsuchinoko."

The laughter in the room grew. Even Naoya felt like he might burst into a fit of giggles. He imagined Takatsuki, dressed in his stylish suit with his trousers rolled up, enthusiastically pushing his way into the tall grass with an insect net in hand.

"In addition, I would go around asking people who live in the area if they have ever seen Tsuchinoko. After all, in the Kanto region, sightings have been reported around the Tama River and in Tsuchiura, but I haven't heard of any out of Yokohama. I would be quite eagerly searching for Tsuchinoko... But then, later on, I find out that the report I had received was made-up."

Takatsuki drew a big X through his Tsuchinoko drawing.

"I would surely be extremely disappointed, having worked so hard to find Tsuchinoko. But there's a bigger problem than my feelings, because thanks to me, incorrect folklore may have taken root in that region."

Takatsuki's shoulders drooped, and he gazed sadly at the Tsuchinoko picture.

"Because I went around asking about it, there could be locals who think *There might be a Tsuchinoko here*. Or *There must be one, if a university professor came here to look for it*. It's possible that, under that mistaken impression, someone could misidentify some other creature as Tsuchinoko and start spreading around that they saw it. If that was to happen, there would be extreme confusion. Because I went to a place where Tsuchinoko was unlikely to be, a legend of it existing there was born without any regional basis or cultural background. My conduct would cause nothing but problems for Tsuchinoko hunters and researchers."

There was no arguing with that. It would be troublesome for plausible rumors of Tsuchinoko's existence to spread in an area where there was no way for it to be found... Regardless of whether "Tsuchinoko hunter" was a real profession or not.

"All this to say, please do not post fictional stories or misinformation on Neighborhood Stories. Also, please don't submit stories you find online. I want you to share stories you've heard firsthand or experienced yourselves. That is my first request. Thank you in advance."

Takatsuki nodded once quickly.

Then, forgoing his clumsy drawing, he turned around to face the class again.

"My second request involves the class format. Basically, lecture topics will be split into two classes. In the introductory class, I will present you with various examples relating to a specific theme. In the second class, which covers commentary, I will explain in detail the connection, roots, cultural background, and so on of the examples introduced in the first lecture. So I'm not sure the commentary will make much sense if you don't hear the introduction. Listening to ninety minutes of exposition on a story you don't know would be a bit tough, right? Accordingly, if you don't attend the introductory lecture, you don't have to attend the commentary one. I'm not saying don't come, but there wouldn't be much point in it. In other words, my second request is 'Please attend as many lectures as you are able.'"

Takatsuki's words had the classroom buzzing with chatter. Even Naoya thought he was being unexpectedly harsh. But then again, it was only natural to expect students to attend every lecture of the classes they had signed up for.

Takatsuki smiled broadly.

"Having said that, you are all college students. This could be the time in your lives that you wish to enjoy the most. Plus, there are part-time jobs, club activities, maybe even relationships to deal with. I'm sure you'll be busy with this and that. Naturally, you may also get sick or have to take a leave of absence for bereavement and so on... Therefore, I will offer make-up classes for students who miss the introductory lectures for whatever reason. They will be held on Fridays during fifth period, but if you can't make that time, please see me in my office. I will give you the materials you missed from the introduction. Of course, the same goes for students who attend the first lecture but miss the commentary."

The talking had yet to die down. Most of it came from the girls in the room. They twittered excitedly over various things—"We can go to Professor Takatsuki's office?" and "Omigosh, do you think he offers one-on-one lessons?"

"Now then, we've covered the course introduction and matters of note. For the remaining time, I'm going to lecture as usual. Since it's our first meeting, I thought it would be best to stick to something more orthodox, so today we're going to talk about the tale of the haunted taxi. This story, which most of you are probably familiar with, is about the seat of a taxi being wet after its passenger disappears. Today will be our introduction, and next week will be the commentary. If you don't think you'll be interested in this theme, feel free to skip next week's commentary lecture. And with that, I'm going to pass out the materials for this topic. Please pass them along to the people sitting behind you."

Saying that, Takatsuki handed a stack of printouts to a student seated in the front row.

There was no one sitting in front of Naoya. Takatsuki came up the first step and handed more printouts directly to him.

The materials contained a variety of articles, including ones published in supernatural-themed periodicals, weekly magazines, and even sports newspapers. Place names, dates, and so on were clearly underlined throughout.

When Naoya handed the stack to the two girls sitting behind him, they glanced quickly at the printouts before looking at each other. They were on the verge of bursting into laughter. Their expressions were part incredulous, part excited. Naoya felt like his face probably looked similar.

For the first time, he thought college might be interesting.

Although, he thought, even more so than college, what was truly interesting was this man named Akira Takatsuki.

*   *   *

As soon as Takatsuki's lecture was over and Naoya left the school building, a barrage of students recruiting for their clubs descended upon him from all sides.

"Are you a first-year? Are you interested in English theater? We'll be performing a portion of *Amadeus* after this in Club Assembly Hall 2A, so please come check it out!"

"We're STEP, the tennis club! Come sweat and stay young with us! We do mixers with other schools! We have a partnership with a famous women's college!"

"We're the film studies club! We do screenings every Friday! If you like independent films, give us a shot!"

"Join the *rakugo* society! Our performance hall is open every day this week starting at five PM!"

Within seconds, Naoya found his hands stuffed full of leaflets, and he was nearly dragged off by someone several times. In a panic, he took shelter in a small alley next to the school building and automatically crammed the leaflets into his bag. He couldn't imagine how it was that the upperclassmen could identify a first-year student on sight. It's not like they wore different-colored badges or indoor shoes in college like they had up through high school.

This part of April was a crucial time for clubs to secure new members. It wasn't so bad in the morning, but in the afternoon, the recruiting efforts exploded. In particular, the area by the campus's main thorough-fare, where clubs had set up registration booths, was bursting with upperclassmen waiting for new students to walk through.

Naoya let out a huge sigh after straightening his disheveled hoodie and glasses. Cutting through that crowd was like diving into a school of piranhas. He had no choice but to go around the back of the school building.

Just as he took a step in that direction, another voice called out.

"Are you a freshman?"

Naoya looked over in irritation at a neatly dressed man and woman.

The female student had spoken to him. Her long black hair was tied back in a single bunch.

"I'm not interested in joining a club."

Naoya's reply took the tone of someone turning down a mall kiosk salesperson. The woman's smile was strained.

"Oh, that's not it. We're not really a club. It's more like... How should I put it? It's a more casual gathering where everyone meets whenever they like—to talk and stuff like that."

"Exactly, a casual gathering. Sometimes we bring a topic to have a little debate over. Or not a debate, just a little chat."

The male student nodded vigorously as he spoke. Naoya didn't trust the pair's pasted-on smiles.

"...If all you do is chat, I don't think you need to invite new members."

This made the male student shake his head as exaggeratedly as he had been nodding it.

"That's not true! Even in a casual setting, new opinions are always needed! Right, for example, what do you think about life? We're born, we grow up, we go to college, enter society, get married, have a variety of experiences, and in the end we die. If that's all there is, what's the point of life?"

"Um, sorry, but I'm not really into philosophy..."

"No, no. It's just a lighthearted question!"

"Right, a casual chat... Look, if you don't join a club in college, it can be hard to find a place to fit in, right? It gets lonely, don't you think? We have a hangout room that any member is free to use. Show up when you want, chat casually with everyone. That's all it is, really. Just a casual gathering."

The two of them had closed in on Naoya while spouting the word *casual* over and over again.

Ah, is that what this is? Naoya thought.

"Is this a religious thing?"

Confronted with such a direct question, the male student's cheeks twitched momentarily.

The woman was still smiling.

"Gosh, where did that come from? **No, we aren't from a religious group.**"

Toward the end of her reply, the female student's voice warped as if she were speaking underwater.

Naoya sighed.

Pulling his earbuds from his bag, he responded:

"…I read somewhere that your face distorts when you lie, but… That's incorrect, isn't it?"

"Huh?"

The woman was looking at Naoya in confusion.

He put his left earbud in.

"I'm not against religion, necessarily. There are people who live by it, and there are some who simply find comfort in it. But I'm not a believer, and I'm not lonely, so I'm fine. Sorry."

With a quick nod, Naoya turned on his heel and walked away. He heard one of them calling out from behind him, but he ignored it, put in his other earbud, and pressed PLAY on his MP3 player. The theme song of a drama that had been popular not so long ago came through the earphones, and the pair's voices soon stopped bothering him.

In the university's orientation materials, there had been a warning about shady religious groups recruiting under the guise of seeking new members for club activities.

Naoya wasn't sure if those two were from that kind of group, but he wasn't interested in following them to find out, and he thought it was underhanded of them to lie when recruiting.

It wasn't right that people's faces distorted when they lied.

The distortion was in their voices.

Although, apparently only Naoya was able to hear it.

At some point, Naoya's ears had gained the ability to hear people's lies as warping in their voices.

When he first heard the distortion, he was utterly bewildered and had no idea why it was happening. He told his parents that sometimes things sounded funny, and at first, they suspected hearing loss. But even though they brought him to one hospital after another, having his ears and even his brain examined, no abnormalities were found.

Then…Naoya figured it out himself.

The only thing that ever sounded distorted was the human voice.

And the only time people's voices ever sounded warped was when they were lying.

Hearing the distorted voices was so unpleasant it made him feel sick when it happened often. But even worse than that was being able to tell every single time someone lied.

Lying came easily to humans. For their own protection, for vanity— people told lies quite easily. They could lie with a straight face, even to those they felt closest to. It was a truth Naoya never wanted to know. The world was full of liars and creaking, warping voices.

Countless times, he thought he would be better off if he just destroyed his eardrums. If he stabbed the core of a pen or an incense stick or something into his ear canal, he wouldn't be able to hear anything anymore, would he? But when he had tried to go through with it, he was seized with fear and just…couldn't.

Maybe, since this ability had started suddenly one day, his hearing might suddenly go back to normal in the future. That optimistic view had faded over the years.

But at the very least, he had learned some coping strategies instead.

If he didn't want to hear something unpleasant, he just put another sound in his ears beforehand instead. Whoever invented the portable music player and earphones was a true genius in Naoya's opinion. The music coming from his earbuds could cancel out most other noise.

And if he didn't want to be hurt every time someone lied—

He just had to build a wall.

Walls between himself and other people. Invisible but definite.

Then, as long as he didn't breach those walls, he was fine.

Blatantly isolating oneself led to various inconveniences, so Naoya avoided that. It was important to talk to others as necessary, smile at them, make safe connections.

But he never got close to anyone.

Crossing that line—befriending someone—he couldn't do it.

Because if he did, and that person lied to him, Naoya would definitely know.

So he had no intention of joining a school club or participating in any "casual gatherings." He would probably have to drop by his classmates' drinking parties at the very least. But that was fine. Shielded by his earbuds and his glasses, he could keep the rest of the world at arm's length. He could tell himself that the ugly day in, day out of lying and being lied to had nothing to do with him.

That female student had said he'd struggle to fit in at college. That he would be lonely.

Naoya didn't feel particularly lonely.

The world inside his walls was always peaceful and calm.

Besides, it wasn't like there was nowhere for him at school. College contained a place that was ideal for those who enjoyed being alone…

The library.

Seiwa University's library was a truly splendid building with eleven stories—eight aboveground and three below. It carried reference materials, periodicals, and videos of all kinds, and there was Wi-Fi. The seats in the reading corner on the first floor, where sunlight shone in through the large windows, were usually mostly filled. But by day three of making regular visits to the library, Naoya noticed that the farther he went below the ground level, the fewer people there were. Perhaps it was because, in addition to the claustrophobic feeling caused by the lower ceilings, the air conditioning was lacking and the air itself was a bit stale, or maybe it was a simple matter of how the books were arranged on the lower floors.

Snagging one of the reading chairs set up along the wall of the second basement level, Naoya took out his smartphone.

He tried searching for the Neighborhood Stories site Takatsuki had talked about.

The site that appeared had a pleasantly neat design. Various urban legends, accompanied by their classifications and examples, were arranged tidily alongside submissions from the general public that had not yet been organized.

A single sentence at the top of the site read:

Please tell me about your neighborhood mystery.

Tentatively, Naoya clicked on the General Submissions page.

He read the most recent post.

```
This was quite a while ago, but I found it
pretty interesting, so I'm sharing. I heard the
woman sitting next to me at the beauty salon
telling this story to her stylist.
   She said it happened when she was a child.
   Around that time, there was a middle-aged man
in black full-body tights who would regularly
appear in her house.
   He didn't really do anything, just ran around
inside the house causing a ruckus. No one in
her family seemed to pay the man any mind,
so she apparently accepted his existence as
normal.
   Then one day, when she came home from elemen-
tary school, she saw the man hanging from the
clothesline as if both his arms had been hooked
around it.
   When she saw him, she thought, Oh no, my mom
washed him.
   "Washed and dried," she said.
   After that, she never saw the man in her house
again.
   Apparently, in her young mind, she thought, He
must have left because he got washed.
   Could the man have been some kind of modern
fairy or something?
```

When he was finished reading, Naoya tilted his head to the side, not sure how to define what he was feeling.

The story had no resolution, although perhaps that was to be expected from a story the poster had merely overheard. And he had no idea what to make of the tale itself.

A middle-aged man in a black bodysuit sounded more like a prank than a specter, but if that man was really a human and not a fairy or a spirit, then he was just a pervert. That was a scary possibility, too. But the fact that the girl's family didn't notice the man pointed to some kind of supernatural presence, after all. It also didn't make any sense that the man disappeared after being laundered.

Naoya wondered how Takatsuki would categorize this story and position it academically.

What he had learned from the first session of Folklore Studies II was that, in college, anything could become a subject for academic study if someone was interested in it.

Naoya took his unfinished schedule out of his bag.

In the third period slot on Wednesday, which he had been leaving blank, he wrote *Folklore Studies II*.

Then he left his seat to look for a library computer where he could use the Collections Lookup service.

Japan's early chronicles and the Edo period encyclopedia Takatsuki had mentioned during his lecture—Naoya suspected the school library would have copies of them all. He wanted to see for himself if they really did contain descriptions of Tsuchinoko.

Akira Takatsuki was quite an interesting character.

Or more to the point, as the course progressed, Naoya gradually came to understand that Takatsuki was a bit of a handsome airhead.

One day, the professor was late for class, which was unusual for him.

Roughly ten minutes after the scheduled start time, Takatsuki rushed into the classroom. He had no sooner switched on the microphone than he started talking.

"Sorry I'm late! I accidentally left a fruit sandwich sitting on my desk in the sun, and I thought it would probably be safe to eat, so I ate it, and it wasn't safe, after all! My stomach was upset, and I ended up stuck on the toilet for a while! I'm so sorry!"

The entire room probably could have done without that announcement.

Another time, during a lecture, Takatsuki drew an incredibly bad diagram of the slit-mouthed woman's various forms on the blackboard. At first, the drawing was just a woman with long black hair and a mask. Then he drew her wearing a red coat and white pants, then with a red hat, and another driving a red sports car. Looking at the collection of pictures, a student sitting behind Naoya whispered, "What the hell? They look like a preschooler's portrait of their mom." It was true. They really did.

Nevertheless, the lectures were interesting and easy to follow. Attendance in other courses had been steadily dwindling, and some were even downgraded from larger rooms to medium-size ones, but Takatsuki's continued to be popular. Even though it didn't fill up as much as it had for the first session, around 80 percent of the lecture hall's seats were occupied for every class.

There certainly were people who skipped Takatsuki's lectures, but... Well, there was one more distinctive trait that the professor had.

They had finished one of their introductory lectures the previous week and were currently engaging in commentary. Takatsuki looked around the room like he did every class. He took notice of some of the students and addressed them.

"You and you, and you three over there, you're here this week even though you missed last week and the supplementary lectures. Are you all right? Should I give you the materials from last week?"

Whether the students were all the way in the front or the back of class, Takatsuki always said the same thing. He probably had great vision, but his memory also appeared to be shockingly good. He remembered who attended each class, even though there were probably more than two hundred students every time.

And by the start of June, Takatsuki was able to remember not only Naoya's face but also his name.

As the lecture was ending and students had begun to get up and leave, Takatsuki switched back on the mic he had just powered off.

"Oh, right, I forgot. Literature Department first-year Fukamachi... Naoya Fukamachi, are you here?"

"...Um, ah, yes! I'm...here."

Suddenly being singled out almost made him jump out of his seat. Takatsuki hadn't called out a student by name like this before. Naoya raised one hand to show he was indeed present.

Takatsuki looked at him.

"I want to speak to you about the report you submitted the other day. Are you free now? If not, you could come to my office another day."

"I-it's fine... I'm free."

Takatsuki nodded and said "Great," then beckoned to Naoya. Reluctantly, Naoya fought through the flow of students trying to exit at the back of the lecture hall and headed for the lectern. It had been a mistake to sit in the back row this time.

Takatsuki had assigned the class a report during the previous lecture. They were told to summarize in their own words one of the subjects they had covered so far. But Naoya didn't know why he was being called forward out of the blue. Had his work been seriously lacking somehow?

By the time he reached the lectern, most of the students had already gone. The classroom was quiet, and Takatsuki was erasing what he had written on the blackboard.

Nervously, Naoya addressed the back of his professor's refined British suit.

"Um, so about my report... Was there something—?"

"Oh, sorry. I must have surprised you, singling you out in front of everyone without warning."

Dusting the chalk from his fingers, Takatsuki turned around.

"Are you able to come to my office now? Do you have any classes after this?"

"I'm done for today. Third period is my last class on Wednesdays."

"Good. Then let's go."

Takatsuki picked up his bag and started walking.

The exit next to the blackboard was primarily for faculty to use, not students. Takatsuki headed for it with a jaunty stride, and Naoya followed him in a hurry.

It was his first time seeing Takatsuki without the distance between the lectern and lecture hall seats between them. Up close like this, it became evident how tall Takatsuki was. Naoya, who was nearly five foot eight, had to look up slightly to meet his eyes. He was probably five foot ten at least. His legs were long, so his stride was big, too. Naoya had to hustle a bit to keep pace with him.

The faculty exit opened directly to the outside. The door Naoya usually left through in the back of the classroom led to the second floor of the school building, but because the lecture hall was tiered, the very front of the room was on the ground level.

Takatsuki spoke as they cut across the sun-drenched courtyard.

"There's no need to be nervous. Your report was well written. You always come to class, and it looks like you take notes. I've been thinking about what an earnest student you are."

He smiled at Naoya.

For a moment, the light flashing in Takatsuki's eyes looked blue. Naoya was stunned.

It wasn't like the bright-blue eyes some Westerners had. It was a darker, deeper color, like the indigo of the night sky.

"Fukamachi? What's wrong?"

Unconsciously, Naoya had been staring at the professor's face, which earned him a puzzled look in response.

Maybe it had only been a trick of the light. Takatsuki's eyes were just a normal shade of brown now.

"Uh, no, it's nothing... Um, Professor?"

"Yes?"

"Do you really remember who attends class each time?"

"I do. My memory has always been slightly above average."

Takatsuki laughed as he answered. Naoya had a feeling he was downplaying things a bit.

It was a chaotic hour to be walking through the courtyard. Club-recruiting efforts died down after April, but regular club activities seemed to have returned in full force. Here and there around the square, groups of students were occupied in various ways. There was a dance club practicing a routine to music, a drama club doing vocal exercises in a circle, quite a large group of people using a big jump rope, and what seemed to be a street-performance society diligently working on juggling.

Takatsuki slipped deftly between them all and walked toward the faculty offices building.

"If there's no problem with my report, why did you want to speak to me?" Naoya asked.

"Ah. Actually, I wanted to ask you about the story you submitted for extra credit," Takatsuki replied.

When he had assigned the report, Takatsuki had told them, "This isn't mandatory, but if anyone submits a strange story they heard from someone else, or a weird experience of their own, I'll give them a few extra points. But as I said before, please don't submit anything fictitious or untrue."

Naoya had written about the mysterious thing that had happened to him as a child.

"To clarify, that wasn't something someone told you—or that you read about somewhere? It happened to you personally?"

"…Yes."

"Right. Well, it was a very interesting story, so if you could tell me a bit—"

Takatsuki froze.

Suddenly, from beside him came the sound of something flapping its wings.

Naoya, also surprised, automatically glanced in that direction.

He saw two pure-white doves just starting to take flight. A pair of students wearing top hats and carrying wands were chasing after them in a panic.

"…That must be the magic club. If they're practicing taking doves out of hats, wouldn't it be better to go indoors…? Professor?"

Naoya paused, noticing that Takatsuki's face had gone horribly rigid.

The professor's bag slipped from his grip. Takatsuki's tall form was trembling. Naoya hastened to reach out and steady him, but he wasn't strong enough to support the other man, and they sank to their knees on the ground together.

"Professor Takatsuki? Professor, are you okay?!"

Looking closer, Takatsuki's downturned face looked totally drained of color. Maybe he was anemic? The nearby students had noticed what happened and were looking at them with concern.

Then, pressing his hands lightly to his own forehead, Takatsuki spoke.

"...Ah, sorry. I didn't mean to scare you."

His voice was weak, but his tone was steady.

"I'll be back to normal in a little while, so don't worry. I'm fine."

"Are you anemic?"

"Well, something like that... I'm afraid of birds."

"Huh? Birds...?"

Some birds *had* just taken off right near the professor.

But...they were just doves.

"Afraid—but why...? Doves don't attack people, sir."

"Even so, I'm scared of birds in general. It's a full-on phobia, actually."

Takatsuki stood as he answered. His complexion was returning to normal, but he still seemed wobbly.

"A phobia...? Why are you so afraid of them?"

"Have you ever seen Hitchcock's *The Birds*, Fukamachi?"

"I haven't."

"You should watch it, then. You'll be afraid of birds, too, for sure."

"Please don't spread your phobia to others."

"No, it's not really the movie's fault. I've always been like this. Sparrows and parakeets and other small birds are fine... Ah, but if there are lots of them, even the small ones are no good. That wing-flapping sound always gets to me."

Takatsuki frowned. He really was terrified of birds. Naoya had heard of conditions like arachnophobia, but he wondered if they were like this—if they made people turn pale and collapse.

"Do you need to go to the infirmary?"

"It's okay; I'll rest in my office."

"Oh, well, then I'll carry your bag."

Naoya reached for the bag that Takatsuki was about to pick up, thinking it was the least he could do.

Surprised, Takatsuki blinked several times as he looked at Naoya, then smiled faintly.

"Thank you, but there are papers and my laptop in there, so it's quite heavy."

"All the more reason for me to carry it."

Naoya lifted the bag, which was just as heavy as Takatsuki had said it would be. Heavy enough that he didn't think someone who was still stumbling a bit should carry it.

He started walking with Takatsuki's bag in hand.

"You're a kind person, Fukamachi. The type who automatically gives up his seat on the train to an elderly person."

"…I'm not particularly kind. That's a normal thing to do."

"It's quite difficult to define *normal*, isn't it? But if you think it's normal to show kindness to someone in trouble, then I think that's a very nice trait to have as a person."

"That's a very scholarly way of saying things."

"Well, I am an academic, in spite of how I may seem now."

Takatsuki smiled more distinctly than before. Perhaps he had recovered a bit.

Takatsuki's office was on the third floor of the faculty building. Because it housed professors and graduate students from every department, first-years didn't have much reason to go inside. On each office door there was a small number plate and a placard with a faculty member's name printed in small letters.

Takatsuki's office was room 304. Apparently, it wasn't locked, because Takatsuki simply pushed open the door and went inside.

Naoya began to follow him—then stopped dead in his tracks in shock.

A person was lying on the floor.

A female student with long hair lay between the large table in the center of the room and the bookshelves along the wall. It looked like she had collapsed there. She was dressed in a baggy top and worn-out jeans. There were books scattered around her, making it look like a crime scene. The girl didn't so much as twitch even when Takatsuki entered the room. One of her fingers was extended on an open book, and Naoya couldn't help but see a victim pointing to her dying message.

"Huh? Uh?! Um, ah, should—should we call an ambulance?!"

"Ah, don't worry. This is the norm for her."

Takatsuki's reply to Naoya's panicked question was calm and unbothered.

"Psst, Miss Ruiko. Haven't I told you before that you shouldn't sleep here? Come on, wake up."

"Hmm...?"

The girl Takatsuki had addressed as Ruiko began to stir when he tapped her on the shoulder.

"Mm... Huh? Professor Akira? Oh no, I fell asleep, didn't I...?"

"Honestly, you can't keep pushing yourself so hard just because you have to present your research soon. If you're having trouble with it, I'm happy to meet with you, so show it to me later, okay? For now, just stop sleeping on my floor. You have marks on your face."

"Ah, I'm sorry. The floor felt so nice and cool..."

Ruiko took Takatsuki's outstretched hand and got up to sit in a nearby metal folding chair. Just as Takatsuki had said, her face had clearly visible marks on it from the seams in the floorboards. She wore red glasses that were sitting at an odd angle, and her long hair, which had been messily tied back, was disheveled. Her face seemed devoid of makeup.

Ruiko turned to look at Naoya. Behind the red frames of her glasses, her eyes blinked vacantly.

"Huh...? Professor Akira? Who's this cutie...? A first-year? What's your name?"

"Oh, um, I'm a first-year in the Literature Department. My name is Fukamachi."

"Oh, really? I'm a first-year, too, in the doctoral program, that is. Nice to meet you; I'm Ruiko Ubukata."

Ruiko gave him a drowsy smile. She looked like she was still half asleep.

Takatsuki was picking up the scattered books off the floor when he chimed in.

"Miss Ruiko, Fukamachi is our guest, so treat him nicely, will you? I'll make you some coffee, so drink it and rest up a bit more—wait a minute. Ruiko, isn't your part-time teaching job today? At the cram school?"

Ruiko startled.

Finally straightening her glasses, her gaze fell on her wristwatch. Her eyes opened wide, and she shot to her feet, her chair clattering with the force.

"Crap, I forgot! Um, ah, I have to go home and change and do my makeup... Okay, I have just enough time! Please excuse me, and thank you so much for reminding me, Professor Akira!"

Grabbing her bag, which had been kicked under the desk, Ruiko left the office like a raging storm. Just like that, she was gone.

Takatsuki directed a wry smile at Naoya, who had stared blankly at Ruiko without thinking as she made her exit.

"Fukamachi, just so you know, she's what we would call a relatively hopeless graduate student. Not all my advisees are like that, okay?"

"Right... Being a graduate student is difficult, isn't it...?"

In any case, Naoya understood very well that Ruiko seemed hopeless in several ways.

"Well, she's a very good, earnest, and enthusiastic kid. And it seems as though living in the lab or the office half the time leading up to their research presentations is just part of being a graduate student. Anyway, sorry for welcoming you with something strange like that, Fukamachi. Please take a seat over there."

Takatsuki took his own bag back from Naoya and set it on the table. He headed for the back of the office.

"Since you came all the way here, I can at least offer you something to drink. What would you like? The options are cocoa, coffee, black tea, and green tea. The teas are in tea bags, and the cocoa happens to be Van Houten!"

"Ah, coffee please."

"The cocoa is really good…"

"I'm not a fan of sweets."

Takatsuki looked at him with genuine disappointment while clutching a Van Houten pouch. Naoya wished he wouldn't.

He wondered if it was okay to have someone who had just been feeling ill make him a drink, but Takatsuki's complexion looked much better already. True to his word, it had only taken him a little while to recover.

Naoya sat in a folding chair and looked around the office.

Takatsuki's office was fairly spacious. In addition to the large table in the center of the room, there were two desks in the corner with laptops on them. The wall facing the door had a big window in it, but the other three were taken up entirely by bookshelves, and the room smelled vaguely like a used bookstore. The shelves contained a mix of technical texts, monthly issues of the occult magazine *MÜ*, and books on urban legends in various subcultures. It seemed quite fitting, for Takatsuki.

In front of the window stood a small table with a kettle and a coffee maker on top. Takatsuki addressed Naoya while retrieving a mug from the cabinet next to the small table.

"Is this the first time you've been in the faculty offices, Fukamachi?"

"Ah, yes… I'm surprised at how much the offices in TV dramas get it right. The atmosphere and such are a lot like this, I think."

"My office is rather plain. Professor Funabashi from the Archeology Department has clay figures and flame-style pottery; Professor Tamura who teaches Western Medieval history has a suit of armor and a lance. In Professor Mitani's office—he teaches Japanese history—there are a bunch of traditional Ichimatsu dolls lined up on the shelves."

"...Is Professor Mitani studying Ichimatsu dolls?"

"No, I think they're just a hobby. There's one in his collection that's half burned and quite terrifying. Apparently, he bought it at a flea market. He says it's harmless, but students are afraid of it and don't like going near his room."

Takatsuki laughed at his own story as he made their drinks.

His voice really was quite pleasant.

It was probably in part due to his gentle and ever-cheerful tone, but even more than that, it helped that Takatsuki didn't tell lies. Granted, Naoya had only ever heard him speak during lectures and while they walked to his office just a little while before, but even so.

Lying was as natural to people as breathing. Even if someone was just lightly embellishing a story to entertain a friend, that was still a lie. But Takatsuki didn't even do that. So it was a pleasant experience, hearing him talk. Naoya would be just fine listening to this voice, even if he had to do it forever.

But as he thought that, another voice spoke up from deep in his heart.

Just because that's true doesn't mean he'll never tell a lie.

That voice whispered to him slyly while he sat trembling with fear.

Sooner or later, he'll lie to you. It's a fact.

Don't trust him. Build your walls. Don't step outside of them.

It's you, after all.

You're—

"Fukamachi?"

Takatsuki's voice suddenly sounded from right beside him.

Naoya looked up in surprise to find the professor standing next to him with a tray in hand. Takatsuki's well-crafted face was peering at him from much too small a distance.

"What's wrong? You look frightened all of a sudden."

"Ah, it's nothing..."

Naoya tried to brush him off, but up close, Takatsuki's eyes seemed to take on that blue tinge again, and for a moment, Naoya's breath caught.

There they were. Deep-indigo eyes the color of the night sky in the countryside.

The exact same shade as the night sky above his grandmother's house—the one he often visited as a child. He used to be afraid that if he looked up at that sky long enough, it would suck him up and cast him into some unknown void.

"Professor, are you biracial or maybe a quarter or something?"

Naoya asked this without thinking, and Takatsuki cocked his head to the side in confusion.

"Hmm? I'm not. Why?"

"Um... Sometimes, your eyes look blue..."

Setting the tray down, Takatsuki's brow furrowed a bit.

"I've been told that before. I don't really know why, myself... Well, iris color depends on the amount of melanin in your eyes. So maybe my eyes have a different amount than most people, and they look blue in the light... Ah, here you go."

He picked up the coffee-filled mug from the tray and gave it to Naoya. The mug was sort of avant-garde, with a multicolored image of the Great Buddha covering its entire surface.

"Why the Great Buddha?"

"Oh, one of my advisees gave that to me as a souvenir from their trip to Nara. You don't like the Buddha, Fukamachi?"

"No, it's not a matter of dislike or anything... Anyway, Professor, um..."

"Hmm? Is something wrong?"

Takatsuki took the seat next to Naoya.

The blue mug in his hand was filled to the brim with cocoa. There were even marshmallows on top. The sweet smell it gave off was enough to make Naoya dizzy.

"You have quite the sweet tooth, sir."

"Brains are only nourished by glucose, after all. It's a good idea to actively consume sugar."

Did that mean Takatsuki regularly drank things that were that sweet? And that he could do so without gaining weight? Well, with a face that sweet, it's not like sugary drinks didn't suit him.

"Now then, Fukamachi, let's get down to business—the story you submitted about that strange experience."

Takatsuki paused to take a sip from his mug and smiled contently.

"Several other students submitted strange stories, but most of them seemed to be taken from the internet or books and modified slightly. But yours wasn't like that. It had the feeling of an actual personal experience to it. That's why I called on you. It was…something like this, wasn't it?"

Takatsuki suddenly looked as if he were staring into the distance.

He started to speak.

"*This happened when I was in elementary school.*

"*Just once, while I was visiting my grandmother's house in the countryside, there was a festival in the middle of the night.*

"*The festival itself was held every year, and I had been looking forward to going. But I caught a fever that year and couldn't go. However, when I awoke in the dead of night, I could hear the thundering of drums, and I thought that the festival must still be in full swing. So I sneaked out of my grandmother's house by myself.*

"*When I got to the festival grounds, all the stalls were closed, and only the festival dance was happening.*

"*Everyone was dancing along to the thundering drums beneath countless blue paper lanterns, which were unlike any I had ever seen before. Oddly, there was no music, and everyone was wearing some kind of face mask.*

"*Come morning, I tried to tell my parents and grandmother about what I saw, but they all told me, 'I don't know what you're talking about. That kind of thing wouldn't happen.'*

"*Maybe it was just a dream, but since it's something strange that I experienced, I'm submitting it just in case.*"

Takatsuki told the story like it was written out in the air in front of him.

Naoya stared at him in shock.

Naoya himself couldn't be sure he remembered exactly what he had written, but he had a feeling it was just as Takatsuki had recited. Possibly even word for word the same.

"Professor, do you remember my entire story?"

"I told you, I have a better memory than most. I can remember something after reading it once."

"Isn't that called, like, instantaneous memory or hyper-memory syndrome?"

Naoya had read about it before. It had come up in a story involving people who could recall everything they saw, heard, and experienced.

"Mm, well, something like that. It's quite convenient and helpful in this profession."

Takatsuki's tone of voice was light. No wonder he always remembered who was in class. And he could probably tell when the other students' submissions were plagiarized because he could recall everything he had read online and in books.

"Enough about me; I'm more interested in your experience, Fukamachi. I have a few questions for you; is that okay?"

"Yes… Though, it happened so long ago, and I don't remember much."

"As much as you remember is fine. So when you say you were in elementary school, how old were you, exactly?"

"I was ten."

"I see. So you weren't extremely young. Old enough to have common sense and intelligence, at least. What part of the countryside were you in?"

"Nagano. A mountain town far from the train station… I don't know where, specifically. I used to visit there every year, but I never paid much attention to the address."

"I'm curious about the phrase you used, '…blue paper lanterns, which were unlike any I had ever seen *before*.' Did you mean that the usual festival lanterns weren't blue?"

"Yes. Regular ones are red, with a shop name or something written in the center... That was the first time I'd ever seen blue ones. And I haven't seen any since then, either."

The year after that incident, Naoya had gone to the festival with his cousins and seen for himself. Among the paper lanterns hanging around the festival site, there was not a single blue one to be found.

Takatsuki nodded, looking deep in thought. He wasn't taking notes, probably because he didn't need to.

"You didn't write in your report about what happened after you got to the festival. Did you stay there dancing with everyone until morning?"

"Ah, no... I didn't dance with anyone. I just...watched from outside the circle. Then, before I knew it, it was morning, and I was back in my futon. That's why I thought maybe it was only a dream."

"Ah, that's a common occurrence. But there must have been something that made you think *That wasn't a dream; it was real*, right?"

Unsure how to answer, Naoya hesitated.

Takatsuki barreled on, taking advantage of Naoya's silence.

"I don't think you would have submitted this story if you thought it was only a dream. There must have been something that made you think it was real. Proof that you were at that festival in the middle of the night. What was it? What made you conclude that it wasn't a dream?"

As expected, Naoya thought, *he's as perceptive as he is intelligent.*

...But how much of the story would Naoya be safe to divulge?

Thinking carefully, Naoya hid his lack of a quick response by taking a drink from his mug. Overlooking the colorful Buddha adorning the mug itself, the coffee didn't taste too bad.

Even if Naoya was to tell someone the unadulterated truth of what happened that night, no one would believe him. Moreover, if he told them everything, he would have to explain about his hearing. And that was the part people would believe the least. It was better not to talk about it.

Naoya put his mug back down and replied.

"When I woke up, there was grass on my pajamas. I had been in bed sleeping ever since my temperature went up, so I couldn't have had grass on me unless I had really gone out alone in the night. That's what made me think it might have been real."

It wasn't a lie. That had happened. It's just—of course—that wasn't the only thing that made Naoya believe he hadn't been dreaming.

"I see..."

Takatsuki looked down a bit and lightly stroked his chin with one hand, as if puzzling over Naoya's words.

Then he asked another question.

"You said all the people dancing were wearing masks on their faces, yes...? What about you? You were wearing one as well, right?"

"How did you know that?"

"I figured you must have been wearing one to attend that festival."

Takatsuki continued.

"I believe what you saw was a festival of the dead."

"The dead...?"

"That kind of dance was originally meant to be a memorial service for the dead and spirits who returned to our world during the late summer. In some regions, people wore various headgear, like masks or straw hats, to hide their faces while dancing. The prevailing theory is that this was done so the otherworldly spirits could join the dance without being noticed. That way, both the dead and the living could have fun together, just during the dance, without any barriers between them. The other theory is that if a spirit sees your face, you'll be taken to the afterlife."

At those words, a chilling sense of dread spread through Naoya's chest.

It's too late. They noticed you.

His grandfather's voice from that night was ringing in his ears.

Naoya tried to shake off the voice. He looked at Takatsuki.

"Professor, do the blue lanterns have some special significance as well?"

"Blue lanterns themselves can be found anywhere, typically. But if you mean the ones at that festival, which usually didn't use them, then

I'm sure there's some meaning there. Speaking of, the color blue brings to mind the blue paper standing lanterns used in storytelling rituals during the Edo period."

"Standing lanterns?"

"Yes. Ghost stories became immensely popular during the Edo period, and storytelling rituals flourished. The rituals involved sharing one hundred ghost stories by candlelight and used wooden-frame standing lanterns covered in blue paper. In the book *Otogibōko*, published in 1666, there's a story called 'If You Speak of Mysteries, the Mysterious Shall Appear,' which documented the customs for storytelling rituals during that time."

Once again, Takatsuki looked as if he was staring off into the distance.

"*The rites of the ritual are thus. On a night absent of moonglow, prepare a wooden lantern, that lantern which be affixed with blue paper, and set fire to the hearts of one hundred candles within. With the telling of each tale, snuff out one candle. Darkness shall fall as the blue light dances, and something frightful shall come to pass...* In other words, on the night of a new moon, they would light one hundred candlewicks inside a standing lantern covered in blue paper—and put out a wick for every story told. The gradual darkness was like a form of theater they could have fun with. I find it very interesting that they were using the color blue at this time. People from that period may have associated the color blue with the underworld."

"The underworld..."

"The world after this one. Sometimes also known as the world where nonhumans live, in contrast to the human world. I think that festival you once attended was absolutely one for the dead. I don't know whether everyone there was dead, or if everyone wore masks so they couldn't tell the living apart from the nonliving. At any rate, I would love to go to that place and gather information."

Takatsuki's eyes shone with a childlike excitement. He brought his mug to his mouth again.

Then, as if something had suddenly occurred to him, he lowered the cup and looked at Naoya.

"Oh, that's right. I have one last question. At that festival, did you eat or drink anything?"

Naoya's shoulders nearly jolted in surprise, but he was fairly sure he managed to hide it.

He looked back at Takatsuki through his glasses and responded.

"Why, um… Why do you ask?"

"Going to a different community and eating their food makes you a part of that community. This exact concept is mentioned in the *Kojiki*. When the mother goddess Izanami died and ate the food of the underworld, she became one of its citizens and could no longer return to our world. If someone at that festival of the dead told you to eat something, and you did—"

"N-no… I didn't! I didn't eat anything!"

The words rushed from Naoya's mouth as he interrupted Takatsuki.

He could practically taste the lingering sticky sweetness on his tongue. In a panic, Naoya took another sip of coffee. Its aroma and bitterness just barely washed away the flavor that lived in his memories.

Takatsuki looked at him dubiously.

"Well…that's good, then."

"…Um. Professor?"

"Hmm? What is it?"

"Why are you so interested in the supernatural?"

Naoya wanted to change the subject.

"I saw your website, Neighborhood Stories. All the entries about ghosts and monsters and spirits and urban legends and such. Do you believe all of them are real?"

"…Naturally, I don't think they're all real, no."

Takatsuki wrapped both hands around his mug as he spoke.

"As I said in class, most tales have a context from which they came to be shared. Either as some kind of warning or moral teaching, or else to explain the inexplicable. In other words, all fables are fabricated… However. What if, amid the fabrication, there are some truths?"

"…Truths?"

"Like testimonials from people who experienced real mysteries or a secondhand account of those incidents... I want to find out if spirits really exist in this world. If they do, of course I want to know. I want to see them, to meet them."

"You have very unique tastes."

"So I've been told."

Takatsuki laughed. His laughing face was truly childlike. If a genuinely innocent child was to grow up without becoming at all jaded, they would become a person like Takatsuki.

"Ah, but you know what? Thanks to my website, I've received tons of stories through general submission. And some of those people come to me directly for advice."

"Advice?"

"People who have had strange experiences want me to help them solve their mysteries. Just recently, this request came in."

Takatsuki reached his arm over the table to retrieve his bag. He took out his laptop and, after clicking a few things, turned it toward Naoya to show him the screen.

It displayed an opened email with a story submitted through the Neighborhood Stories submission form. The sender, a woman, had written that the apartment building she lived in might be haunted, and she wanted Takatsuki to come check it out.

"A haunted building..."

"It's not very detailed, but it seems like something might come of it, right? I'd really like to go!"

Takatsuki's eyes were gleaming.

"Then what are you planning to do about this, Professor?"

"Well, I'm thinking I want to go hear the full story and investigate."

"Do you have psychic abilities or something like that?"

"Not in the slightest, unfortunately. But I can investigate anyway."

He seemed to mean what he was saying. Come to think of it, he had said he would go looking for Tsuchinoko if he got a report about it. Maybe academics were just oddballs, after all.

In any case, it seemed the questions about Naoya's report were over. He felt like it was time to leave. The subjects they were just talking about had nothing to do with him.

Finishing his coffee, Naoya grabbed his bag and stood up.

"Well, I should go—"

But he was stopped short.

"Wait, Fukamachi! I just had a great idea!"

Takatsuki caught hold of Naoya's hand.

Naoya stared down in surprise at his professor, who was still clutching Naoya's hand as he got out of his chair. In an instant, he found himself looking up at the other man instead, their roles reversed. Naoya had no idea what was going on, but Takatsuki's eyes were as bright as ever as they gazed down at his upturned face.

"Hey, Fukamachi, would you like a part-time job?"

"P-part-time job?"

"Yes. Assisting me, to be specific. When I go to meet the person who emailed me asking for help, I'd like you to come, too."

Takatsuki smiled cheerfully, Naoya's hand still in his grasp. What on earth was he saying, all of a sudden?

"Wh-why me...? I'm not qualified to be an assistant! One of your graduate students would be so much more helpful. Like that girl from before."

"Well, they're all busy. Besides, you don't need any type of special skills, because I've got that covered. What I need is common sense."

"...Pardon?"

"I have this problem, you see. Oftentimes, I severely lack the same sort of common sense that most people have."

Naoya wished Takatsuki hadn't just said something so ridiculous with such a genuinely troubled expression. And besides that, Naoya needed him to let go of his hand, stat.

"The other thing is: Whenever I go somewhere new for the first time, I always get lost."

"Why don't you just use a map?"

"I do use a map! But maps don't have that much information on them, do they? They show roads and buildings, but when you actually go somewhere, there are other things, too, you know? Vending machines, bicycles parked in street parking, shop signs, products lined up outside storefronts, pedestrians and their dogs. When I take in all those sights at once, my brain gets overloaded, and I can't compare things to the map..."

Takatsuki lightly tapped his temple with his finger.

Evidently, this was a case of his extraordinary memory becoming a hindrance.

Ordinary people saw only what they needed or wanted to see when looking at a single scene. Their brains unconsciously sorted through information and either threw out what wasn't necessary or supplemented information where called for. However, Takatsuki's brain likely recorded everything that entered his field of vision to memory, clearly and immediately. It was probably difficult for him to reconcile the flood of information with the overt simplicity of an everyday map.

"Therefore, the traits I look for in an assistant are common sense and not getting lost. I wonder, Fukamachi, are you a sensible person who can read a map?"

"...Yes, more or less."

"Then it's decided! I'll arrange things around your schedule; so when are you free?"

Takatsuki went from—still—just clutching Naoya's hand to giving him a vigorous handshake with a beaming smile. Maybe he really was a bit lacking in sense, given how he had just decided on things all by himself.

Nonetheless, Takatsuki followed it up by offering him a pay rate that was nothing to sneeze at, and after considering the state of his finances, Naoya accepted the professor's proposal.

And so, that very weekend, Naoya went with Takatsuki to meet the woman who said she lived in a haunted apartment building.

The woman was an office worker living in Suginami ward named Nanako Katsuragi.

They had arranged to meet Nanako at a café that was a minute's walk from Asagaya Station. Naoya figured that even Takatsuki would be able to navigate that much, but just in case, he told the professor he would meet him in front of the station ticket gate.

It turned out to be the right decision.

"...Professor, not that way."

"Oh, this isn't the right way?"

Naoya had tried letting Takatsuki take the lead but had hurriedly stopped him once Takatsuki began walking in the exact wrong direction. If his very first step was a miss, he was guaranteed to get lost.

"Professor, how on earth have you managed to survive this long?"

"I've met many kind people in my life."

Takatsuki met Naoya's exasperated look with a smile.

"But once I've walked around a place once, I always remember it, so it's fine. I only get lost the first time."

"What would happen if, say, a few years pass, and the landscape of the area changes?"

"Ah, surprisingly I can handle that. Even if some buildings are renovated or the shops change, as long as the roads mostly stay the same, some sort of consistency is maintained. Like, how if you look at old black-and-white photos and compare them to modern ones of the same place, you can recognize some aspects, right? It's like that."

"So that's how it is... Well, for now, please don't walk ahead of me until you have the area memorized, Professor. I'll lead."

That settled, Naoya headed for the meeting place with an admirably apologetic Takatsuki in tow.

As they entered the café, a woman seated in the middle of the shop looked over at them. She met Takatsuki's eyes and bobbed her head slightly. *She must be Nanako Katsuragi,* Naoya thought. She had probably looked up Takatsuki's face online or something beforehand.

Nanako Katsuragi had shoulder-length straight hair and a meek disposition. She looked to be in her late twenties or early thirties.

As they sat down next to each other across from her, Nanako nodded once more at Takatsuki.

"I'm Katsuragi. Thank you for meeting with me."

"I'm Takatsuki. This is my student, Fukamachi. He'll be helping me." Takatsuki handed her his business card.

With his features so elegantly arranged, when he smiled softly and spoke intelligently, he seemed like such a reliable person. In reality, he was a hopeless guy who couldn't even find a place that was just a minute's walk from the train station on his own.

When a server came, Naoya ordered coffee, and Takatsuki asked for cocoa. Once their drinks arrived at the table, Takatsuki turned his attention to Nanako.

"Now, could you tell me more about your situation?"

Nanako nodded and began speaking in a faint voice.

"My apartment building... There's something off about it, somehow..."

Nanako explained that she had moved into her apartment about two months prior. It was a small studio apartment on the second floor. The building was old, but the interior seemed to have been renovated recently, and the apartment was fairly clean.

One month after moving in, late at night, she had noticed something strange for the first time.

She heard a steady rapping sound—*knock, knock. Knock, knock.* Not from the front door, but from the wall. It seemed like the person living in the apartment next door was tapping on their shared wall.

She had ignored it at first. However, it went on for days, and she hadn't been able to stand it anymore. One day, Nanako finally went to confront her neighbor.

But no matter how many times she knocked on their door, no one came to answer it.

There hadn't been any other signs of life from that apartment, and the nameplate was blank. The next morning, she had gone to see the landlord, who confirmed that the unit was unoccupied.

When Nanako insisted that surely there had to be someone living there, the landlord understandably looked concerned. Without needing to be asked, he went with Nanako to check the unit, thinking it was possible that someone had moved in without permission.

"But…the locks hadn't been picked; the windows were intact. The apartment, too—it didn't look as if anyone was living there."

The landlord had left after telling Nanako she was just exhausted from having moved recently. Nanako herself supposed it couldn't be anything more than that after seeing the apartment for herself.

But the knocking continued.

As time passed, in fact, the sound changed from a knock to the *scriiitch, scriiitch* sound of fingernails raking down the wall.

"I'm afraid…but my landlord won't do anything to help. Because he says the apartment is empty."

She really wanted to move. But after relocating several times already, she couldn't afford to do it again.

And the mystery had only gotten stranger.

One day after coming home from work, Nanako found a long strand of hair in her room that clearly wasn't hers.

Another time, she found a handprint smeared on the outside of the glass door to the balcony. Her second-floor balcony.

"That's when I thought that maybe someone died in this apartment before, so perhaps it's cursed."

"In other words, you thought it might be a stigmatized property?"

Nanako nodded at Takatsuki's words, her face tormented.

"I mean, I couldn't think of another explanation. If the curse was on me instead of the property, scary things would be happening in other places, too, right? But whenever something happens, it's always in my apartment!"

"However, stigmatized properties are considered to have psychological flaws, and that must be disclosed prior to signing. Your realtor didn't inform you of anything like that before you signed the lease, did they?"

"No, they didn't. But I had to know, so I went directly to the agency that listed my apartment to ask."

The realtor who had helped her just happened to be there, so Nanako explained what had been going on in the apartment and asked him whether some kind of incident had occurred there.

He had replied, "That unit is not what I would call stigmatized."

But his demeanor had been a bit strange. His answer had been vague and evasive, as if he was trying to hide something—or at least, that's what Nanako thought.

After talking with him, her suspicions only grew.

Something violent must have happened in her apartment.

It must be haunted.

Nanako had never really believed in ghosts before.

But she wasn't sure how else to explain what had been happening to her. She went to a shrine to be purified and bought charms and talismans to place around her apartment, but none of it worked. She tried pleading with her landlord, but he got angry and told her to "stop being ridiculous." He even said "If you start spreading strange rumors around, I'll kick you out," even though Nanako would have already left on her own if she were able. She even considered hiring a psychic or a shaman, but she didn't know where to go for that, and she was afraid that if she found one on the internet, she wouldn't be able to tell if they were authentic.

Then one day, Nanako heard about Takatsuki from a work friend. Her friend told her there was an associate professor at Seiwa University who was collecting and investigating strange stories.

She could be sure that a college professor wasn't a fraud, and maybe he could explain what was happening in her apartment.

Desperately clinging to that thought, Nanako contacted Takatsuki.

"Please, Professor. Please help me. I feel like I'm going crazy...!"

Nanako bowed her head to Takatsuki as she made her plea. Her voice was so distraught that the other customers in the café were looking around at them curiously.

Seeing Nanako that way, Naoya frowned.

Because so far, there hadn't been a single lie in her story.

Her voice had been frightened and trembling at times, but it hadn't warped or creaked even once. Everything she had just said had really happened.

If that was true, then—was this a genuine haunting?

Takatsuki spoke up.

"Please raise your head, Miss Katsuragi. I understand what you're saying."

Then he stuck out his right hand toward Nanako, as if he were asking for a handshake.

Lifting her head, Nanako timidly reached for him.

When she did, Takatsuki grasped her hand tightly in both of his.

"Oh! Ah, um…?"

Surprised, Nanako tried to withdraw her hand.

But Takatsuki was holding on to her enthusiastically and didn't let go.

"Miss Katsuragi, I'm so glad I met you. This must be fate."

"Wha…?"

Takatsuki was bent over the table eagerly, staring intensely into Nanako's eyes, looking like he was about to confess his love as he murmured to her.

Nanako's cheeks burned red as she looked back at him. Evidently, she had only just realized that the man sitting in front of her was surprisingly handsome. Her eyes, which had been clouded with tears of worry and anxiety only moments before, began to sparkle for a different reason.

"Miss Katsuragi, can I tell you, frankly, how I'm feeling right now?"

"Uh, ah, that's— I'm— I don't know if I'm ready… Wh-what is it?"

"I am so envious of you."

"…I beg your pardon?"

Eyes fixed on Takatsuki, Nanako tilted her head to the side in confusion. She seemed aware that she had just heard something that didn't fit this situation, but her head hadn't caught up yet.

Takatsuki leaned even closer to her.

"Ah, truly! From the bottom of my heart, I envy you! I wish I could switch places with you right now and live in that wonderful apartment myself! A stigmatized property, spectral disturbances! That's the kind of place that stimulates my intellectual curiosity! Miss Katsuragi, please allow me to investigate the mysteries in your apartment! Right, first, would it be okay for me to see the inside of it? Ah, how exciting, I wonder if any ghosts will appear! I can't wait!"

Takatsuki, still clutching Nanako's hand, shook it vigorously up and down as he spoke.

Nanako had been smiling vaguely, but her face was gradually being overcome with a look of discomfort. *This is bad*, thought Naoya. She was clearly shutting down. The looks from the other customers were embarrassing, too. Takatsuki was talking far too loudly about a topic that was very unusual.

Naoya realized, as the person with common sense, that this might be his time to intervene, so he whispered quietly into Takatsuki's ear.

"Professor, please calm down. Your voice is too loud."

"Calm down? How could I, Fukamachi? Haven't you been listening? There are ghosts in her apartment! This is wonderful!"

It was no use. This thirty-four-year-old could not read the room. He looked more and more like a golden retriever Naoya had owned years before. He was just like a dog, tail wagging and eyes sparkling, standing in front of his favorite toy.

"P-Professor, let's just speak a little more quietly. The other customers are looking at us, okay? And I think it's time you let go of Miss Katsura-gi's hand, yes? Come on, quickly. Let it go."

"Huh? Why, Fukamachi?! What a strange kid you are, telling me to let go of this lovely lady's hand!"

Naoya had tried calming down Takatsuki gently, but his tail wagging didn't subside in the least. Like a dog that jumped up and barked at passersby on a walk. The eyes of those around them were becoming ever more focused on their table. Flustered, Naoya grabbed hold of Takatsuki's arm without thinking.

"Ugh, enough already! Hurry up and let her go! And look around you! Don't shout inside a shop with this many other customers in it!"

He scolded Takatsuki, his tone low, forgetting that he was speaking to an associate college professor.

Takatsuki came to his senses with a start.

He hurriedly released Nanako's hand, sat back down properly in his chair, and looked nervously around the room. Noticing the other patron's inquiring looks, he hunched his shoulders into himself, withdrawing.

"...I-I'm sorry, Fukamachi, Miss Katsuragi..."

He spoke dejectedly, his expression just like that of a chided dog. This situation definitely would have been difficult without a sensible person tagging along, after all.

To fulfill his duties as the sensible one, Naoya began to lecture the crestfallen Takatsuki.

"Listen, Professor. This is stressful enough for Miss Katsuragi. It's fine to investigate, but I don't think you should say you're excited or looking forward to it."

"...I understand. I'm sorry."

"Also, you're old enough to know better than to bother the people around you by yelling. And it's not okay to grab a woman's hand like that the first time that you meet her. I mean, what were you thinking, grabbing her hand with such familiarity? Are you an American?"

"I'm sorry. I would've even hugged her if given the chance."

"You can't. Hug culture hasn't caught on in Japan yet. You'd be labeled a pervert."

"...I wouldn't mind being hugged, though, if it was by Professor Takatsuki."

Nanako interjected in a low voice.

"Miss Katsuragi! You too?! Now's not the time to say 'As long as he's attractive,' don't you think?"

"Ah, right, sorry..."

At Naoya's words, Nanako shrank inward just like Takatsuki.

Wondering why he, as the youngest person at the table, was scolding two grown adults, Naoya thought about the rest of their plans for the day and felt like he was at his wit's end. Things were really looking bleak.

Nanako's apartment was about ten minutes away from the train station.

The building itself was utterly normal and situated in a quiet residential neighborhood. Despite being fairly old, it didn't have the air of a haunted house. There were six units in total in the two-story complex. According to Nanako, four of the six apartments were occupied.

Nanako's was the rearmost unit on the second floor. The only wall of her apartment that she shared with the neighboring unit was the right-side one. Incidentally, the resident of the first apartment was a male office worker who apparently traveled a lot for his job and tended to be away, although he did stay at home sometimes.

They decided to start by seeing the inside of Nanako's apartment.

"Ah, this is a nice place."

Takatsuki looked around the room approvingly. He seemed to have forgotten the shock of being scolded on the walk from the café. His voice was back to its usual cheerfulness.

And as he'd said, the apartment was nice. Compared to the building's shabby exterior, the inside clearly had the look of being recently remodeled. There was wooden flooring and even new wallpaper.

"The realtor said it was renovated. The floors used to be straw mat, and the walls were old, too, I guess. But they made everything nice and clean... Although that just makes me suspicious of why all that was necessary. I'm sure it makes it easier to find tenants, but what if there were bloodstains or something..."

Fear seemed to increase people's power of imagination. It certainly had done so for Nanako.

"Miss Katsuragi, is this the wall where you heard the knocking and scratching?"

Takatsuki pointed at a wall that had a bed pushed up against it.

"Yes, that's the one. I could hear the knocking when I was sitting in bed at night relaxing... Lately, I've been putting in earbuds and listening to music when I'm in bed."

"I see. Ah yes, the walls certainly do seem thin."

Leaning over the bed, Takatsuki rapped on the wall.

Then he looked toward the glass door at the back of the unit that led to the balcony.

"Where exactly was the handprint?"

"About here... It creeped me out, so I wiped it off right away, unfortunately. Oh, and it wasn't a blood print or anything, just the normal smear a hand makes when you push against something."

The spot Nanako had pointed to was approximately the height of her face. All that was in that spot now were a few lingering traces of the rain that had fallen the day before.

Takatsuki threw open the glass door, slipped on the outdoor slippers that had been placed there, and stepped outside. From the doorway, Naoya also surveyed the state of the balcony. Not that there was much to see. It was a normal balcony with nothing on it, probably used only as a place to hang laundry. The neighboring unit's balcony was partitioned off by what looked like a thin piece of sheet metal.

"That's a cherry tree, isn't it? It must be nice to be able to see the cherry blossoms from inside your apartment in the spring!"

Takatsuki spoke, looking at the tree that was growing right outside the balcony. It was planted in the garden of the nearest lot.

Nanako smiled wryly at his words.

"Yes, it was beautiful right around when I moved here. It's nice, but it's quite a large tree, so it does block the sun from my room a bit..."

"Ah, of course. Although, it might be nice to be shaded from the sun's rays in the summer, no? And the branches spread out quite nicely here, so you don't need blinds to protect you from prying eyes."

"That's true... I don't know if I'll still be living here in the summer, though."

Nanako's tone was gloomy.

Takatsuki smiled.

"It's all right. If this property really is haunted, I'll live here instead, as I said before. You can live in my condo, Miss Katsuragi. And if the ghosts aren't real—once we uncover the source, the strange things will stop."

They decided to check out the neighboring apartment next.

Evidently, the building's landlord lived nearby, but he was out running errands for the day. Luckily, Nanako had spoken to him ahead of time, and he'd told her he left the key to the unit with the real estate agent.

The agency was called Mitsuhashi Housing. The three of them stopped into the agency office near the station. As it happened, there were no other customers, and the man behind the counter saw them and stood up as they entered. He was a solidly built man in his thirties with a friendly face.

"Hello, Miss Katsuragi! I heard from Mr. Hayashida. Please come in."

The man's voice was a little high-pitched for his body. The "Mr. Hayashida" he mentioned must have been the landlord.

Before Nanako could move, Takatsuki stepped up to the counter and sat down in the chair opposite the other man.

The man stared at him in surprise.

"Um, you are…?"

"Hello. My name is Takatsuki. I'm investigating what's going on in Miss Katsuragi's apartment, at her request."

Smiling amiably, Takatsuki took out a business card and handed it over.

"Wh-why, a college professor… Oh, excuse me. My name is Yamaguchi. I was the realtor who helped Miss Katsuragi secure her apartment."

The man—Yamaguchi—took out his own business card for Takatsuki to have in return.

Takatsuki accepted it with a smile.

"Then, Mr. Yamaguchi, allow me to get straight to the point. Has anyone died in that apartment—or in the one next door?"

"P-Professor Takatsuki!"

His words were much too direct, and Naoya wanted to jump in as the sensible one. If Yamaguchi reacted badly to Takatsuki's rudeness, they'd be in trouble.

But suddenly, for some reason, Yamaguchi's face stiffened, and he glanced quickly toward the back of the office.

There was someone else there—a woman with long hair who seemed to be the office administrator. She was peering questioningly toward them.

Yamaguchi stood up quickly, grabbed his bag, and called toward the woman.

"Ms. Miura! I'm heading out for a minute! If anything comes up, call my cell."

Then he hurriedly ushered them all out of the office.

As they were walking away from the building, Yamaguchi let out a big sigh.

"...Even without other customers around, it's a bit problematic for you to talk about such things in the office. Our office manager is still fairly new. It'll hurt our reputation if you cause a weird misunderstanding and spread strange rumors around."

"I apologize for that. But from the look of things, you know something about this situation, don't you?"

Takatsuki didn't look the slightest bit apologetic.

And Yamaguchi's attitude certainly was a little odd. Naoya had to assume he knew something about Nanako's apartment.

"Mr. Yamaguchi... I asked you the other day, but you know something, don't you? If you do, please tell me. Please," Nanako said.

Yamaguchi looked down, his face troubled, and sighed again.

Then, in a small voice, he said, "I'm sorry. There are a lot of people here, so... Let's talk when we get to the apartment. I have the keys."

The room in question—the one next to Nanako's—really did seem unoccupied.

There were no signs of anyone living there, and it was totally empty. It looked like it was cleaned regularly and hadn't been messed up. The layout was the same as Nanako's. This apartment had also recently been renovated, it seemed.

"...When Miss Katsuragi signed her lease, I didn't inform her of any psychological flaws. Because there aren't any...in *her* apartment."

Clutching the key to the empty unit, Yamaguchi dropped his gaze to the floor and spoke in a hushed voice.

Nanako looked around the room anxiously.

"Does that mean, um, is...is this apartment...?"

Yamaguchi nodded slightly in response.

At that, she let out a panicked scream and clung to Takatsuki's arm at her side. Without really knowing why, Naoya also scanned the room. It wasn't like he was going to be able to see a ghost or anything, but having just been told this place was stigmatized, he didn't feel comfortable being in it.

Still holding on to Takatsuki for support, Nanako spoke again.

"Why didn't you tell me before I signed the lease?! That's so unfair!"

"Miss Katsuragi, there's no obligation for him to tell you the adjacent unit is a stigmatized property. And your apartment isn't stigmatized, so that means he didn't lie to you when you asked before."

Takatsuki's tone was calm.

Then, with Nanako hanging from his sleeve, he turned to Yamaguchi.

"Was it suicide? Or murder?"

"It was...**suicide**."

Suddenly, Yamaguchi's voice warbled and warped.

Naoya looked at him, startled.

As ever, Yamaguchi was looking at the floor. He kept on talking in a low voice.

"It was a young woman. She had long hair... Her lover had broken up with her. Then she tied a cord to that lintel and hanged herself..."

He pointed to the lintel, but it looked pristine. Yamaguchi explained that it had been replaced during the remodel. But his explanation also came out horribly warped and mixed up.

"But that happened over four years ago now. People have rented this apartment for short periods of time since then. That's why our agency doesn't consider this unit a stigmatized property **anymore**."

"Ah, generally in cases of suicide, the obligation to disclose psychological defects lasts for up to two years. There's also an obligation to disclose to whoever first leases the property following the suicide, but it's not necessary to do so with the tenant following that. In other words, Mr. Yamaguchi's conduct as a realtor is acceptable," Takatsuki said.

Yamaguchi bowed his head toward Nanako, looking truly apologetic.

"We had the apartment properly purified. But the person who rented it immediately after the suicide did say strange things were happening and moved out after a short while... We had another purification performed at that time. Beyond that, there isn't much my agency can do."

Covering one of his ears with his hand, Naoya wondered what on earth was going on.

Everything Yamaguchi said was a total lie. Which meant no young, long-haired woman had died by suicide in this apartment.

But then why was Yamaguchi lying about it?

And if this apartment wasn't stigmatized anymore, then what was the bizarre phenomenon that Nanako was experiencing in hers?

All Naoya knew was which things other people were lying about. He couldn't tell what their reason for lying was—or what truths were being concealed by their lies.

Naoya scowled at Yamaguchi, feeling a bit irritated. He wanted to grab the man by his collar and demand that he tell the truth, but there was no way he could do that. Because when he told people he could hear lies, they didn't believe him.

Then suddenly, Naoya felt someone staring at him.

Glancing quickly over his shoulder, he found Takatsuki's gaze on him for some reason.

He shot his professor a questioning glance, as if to say "What is it?" But Takatsuki just smiled as though it was nothing.

"I see, so a woman passed away in this room! Then it may be safe to assume that's the cause of the mysterious things happening in Miss Katsuragi's apartment, don't you think?"

When he was done talking, Takatsuki began heading energetically toward the back of the room. Nanako, still holding tight to Takatsuki until then, seemed about to follow suit. But maybe the idea of walking near the spot where someone died by suicide was too much, because she released Takatsuki's arm and stayed put.

"Miss Katsuragi's apartment is on the other side of this wall, right? Her bed should be somewhere around here. You said it was a knocking sound—like this?"

He tapped on the wall, *knock, knock.*

Nanako nodded.

"Yes, it was like that. That sound, repeated over and over again."

"I see. And the scratching sound? The *scritch, scritch?*"

Takatsuki went to scratch at the wallpaper like a cat.

Yamaguchi stopped him immediately.

"Hey, don't do that! If you damage the wall, you'll have to fix it!"

"Ah, apologies. Of course, I won't actually scratch the wall."

Takatsuki had that much sense, at least.

But the words he said next were baffling.

"But this wall…it's already damaged, no?"

"Huh?"

Yamaguchi gaped in surprise.

Takatsuki beckoned them forward.

"Look, here. See for yourself."

Yamaguchi approached him, followed by Naoya. Not wanting to be left standing alone, Nanako trailed along timidly.

At first glance, the patch of wall Takatsuki had indicated didn't look damaged.

"Here, look ve-e-ery closely. Ah, maybe it's easier to see at an angle, depending on the lighting? It's here, right here."

Everyone craned their necks.

Nanako let out a small *"Oh."*

Just as Takatsuki had said, there were faint white lines on the wall. Three of them, vertical, more like slight dents than scratches. Long marks left on the wallpaper.

"H-how did this...?"

Yamaguchi's words came out in a groan. Looking frightened, Nanako clung to the nearest arm again, which happened to be Yamaguchi's this time.

Naoya looked at the marks with suspicion. Yamaguchi's story about a woman dying by suicide here was a lie. So who had made these scratch marks?

Her voice trembling, Nanako spoke.

"B-but this doesn't make sense! The scratching noise I heard was so loud... I really don't think it would have left such faint lines... Unless the noises were loud because it was supernatural activity, after all?"

"Well, who can say? But at least this proves the scratching sounds weren't just your imagination, Miss Katsuragi. Things are getting more and more interesting!"

Takatsuki's smile was unsuitably cheery for the situation.

It was probably only Takatsuki who found it so interesting, though no one said so aloud.

The next thing Takatsuki did was gather information in the area. He went looking for anyone who knew anything about the "long-haired woman who died by suicide" either before or after her death.

Yamaguchi had to return to work, so Takatsuki, Naoya, and Nanako decided to speak to people living in the neighborhood themselves.

Nanako informed them that, other than her landlord, Mr. Hayashida, she didn't really know that many people in the area. She greeted them on the street in passing, but that was all. Therefore she was a little hesitant to go asking around the area, but Takatsuki did not seem to share that compunction at all.

"Hello! Do you have a minute to talk?"

Smiling, he approached passersby and began talking to them as he pleased.

Oddly enough, very few people ignored him and walked away. Takatsuki's handsome face and gentlemanly atmosphere worked in his favor. It worked especially well on housewives. While he was talking to one, two or three others would come gather around them.

"What? Someone died in that building? Hmm... I just moved into this neighborhood recently. I don't know about things that happened over four years ago."

"Yes, same here."

"Aren't most of the people who live in that building unmarried and working full-time during the day? They don't really socialize much with us, you know."

All the homes in the area were new, and upon asking, they found out that the neighborhood had become a residential area three years before.

Naoya took his chances in asking a direct question.

"Do you ever see people other than the residents of the apartment building going in and out of there?"

But he didn't get the answer he was hoping for.

"I'm not sure... I only vaguely recognize the faces of the people who live there. Delivery and salespeople come and go as well, of course."

That was what it was like, living in an urban neighborhood. Well, even Naoya didn't really talk to the other people living in his apartment complex—and only dimly recalled what they looked like. If something was to happen nearby and the police came to speak to him, he wasn't confident he would be able to give them a sufficient statement.

Nanako hadn't been lying. The knocking and scratching sounds she heard were real. Her story was corroborated by the scratch marks in the neighboring apartment.

So the question was: Who put those marks there? And how? The apartment was typically locked, and it wasn't like someone could go in and out of it as they pleased.

Since Yamaguchi's suicide story was a lie, it had to be a living person who was responsible for everything—although, it occurred to Naoya, there was one other possibility.

Even if the young woman's suicide was a lie, someone else could have died some other way. The possibility of a ghost haunting the apartment couldn't be ruled out.

After all, Naoya could hardly state with conviction that ghosts did not exist.

"Did someone die in that building...? Well, naturally."

Only one of the people they spoke to made any mention of a death in the apartment—a squat older woman.

She told them she lived in a very old house a little ways from the apartment building. "My back may be crooked, but my mind isn't," she said.

Takatsuki crouched down to meet her at eye level and spoke to her politely.

"So you knew the person who passed away there?"

"Not personally."

The woman snorted with a huff.

"But that building has been there for about twenty years. It's been remodeled several times, but it's not like they rebuilt the structure itself. There are bound to be ghosts in a place that's been around that long."

"What do you mean by that?"

"The spirits of the dead can appear anywhere, you see."

The woman snorted again.

Then, with her cane, she pointed at a house slightly up the way.

"That house. The older lady who lived there died ten years ago. Heart attack, apparently. In the house across the street, the wife died twelve years ago. I think she fell down the stairs. Down that road over there, a child was hit by a car eight years ago and died... People make a lot of fuss over stigmatized properties or what have you, but if you ask me, there isn't a piece of land in this world where no one has died. Going back in time, there were people killed in war, people who collapsed in the street, and I'm sure primitive people were killed by animals all the time. We all live on top of dead people, so to speak. I mean, not just people. If you think about other creatures, too, there are corpses everywhere."

In the end, no one other than the old woman mentioned anything about a death in the apartment building.

But for Nanako, who had believed Yamaguchi's story from the beginning, there hadn't been any need to ask around the neighborhood in the first place. Someone had died by suicide in the apartment next to hers, and for some reason her apartment was the one being haunted. She seemed convinced of it.

She was utterly terrified, so Takatsuki gave her a suggestion.

"Why don't we do this, Miss Katsuragi? Allow me to stay in your apartment, just for tonight."

"...What?"

"I'll stay in your apartment tonight. And if something supernatural is happening, I'll confirm it. Of course, I can't spend the night alone with a young lady in a single bedroom, so it would be best for you to stay somewhere else... Do you have somewhere you can go? You said your parents live far away, I believe, so maybe a friend's house? Or if nothing else, a hotel."

"Oh... Um, let me ask a friend."

Nanako took out her cell phone to make a call.

While she did that, Takatsuki turned to Naoya.

"Fukamachi, you can leave as well. I've memorized the roads around here and won't get lost anymore, and I don't think I'll need common sense for dealing with ghosts."

"... No, I've accompanied you this far, so I'm going to see this through to the morning."

Takatsuki's eyes widened a bit at Naoya's reply.

"Huh, really? Are you sure?"

"I'm sure. I don't have anything to do tomorrow...and telling me you don't need me here anymore, I can't help but be concerned."

After all, Naoya wanted to know, too. What was happening in Nanako's apartment?

On top of that, if Yamaguchi's lies had something to do with things... By himself, Takatsuki could be in danger if something was to happen. Two people were usually better than one, right?

Takatsuki's face broke out in a pleasant smile; he looked just like a friendly dog.

"You really are kind, Fukamachi. Accompanying me—and even staying with me overnight."

"Like I said, it's not that I'm especially kind. I'm just in too deep to turn back now."

"That's not true. You could stop here, but you aren't going to, because you're a good person... Okay! Then, after this, let's go buy food and snacks for tonight's sleepover! I'll pay, so you can get whatever you want!"

"It's not a sleepover?! And buying snacks—are you crazy? How much are you enjoying this?!"

"What? Isn't it important to find the joy in anything we do?"

As always, Takatsuki looked like a dog with his tail wagging happily as he spoke. Thinking about it, Naoya had a feeling that Mr. Associate Professor here had been called crazy many times, but since he didn't seem to mind, it was probably fine.

Having decided to stay with a friend for the night, Nanako returned to her apartment to pack an overnight bag. Takatsuki and Naoya saw her to the train station.

The sun would be setting soon. The road outside the station was starting to fill up with people who were returning from work or shopping. Everyone had somewhere to call home. It would be unbearable for that home to be threatened by ghosts or some other unknown force.

No matter what was happening in Nanako's apartment, it would be nice if Takatsuki and Naoya could solve it during their overnight stay, but...would they succeed? To begin with, there was a chance nothing would happen unless Nanako was present.

Suddenly, Takatsuki was calling out and waving his arm.

"Ah, Mr. Yamaguchi! Are you going home?"

Looking in the direction Takatsuki was waving, on the other side of the crowd of people, sure enough, Naoya saw Yamaguchi's face. Even with this many people around, he was easily recognizable. Yamaguchi looked around with a surprised expression, then walked toward them.

"Ah, everyone. I'm sorry about earlier... Did you find anything out after I left?"

"Yes, well, I learned that all the married ladies in the neighborhood are very nice and easy to talk to."

"Excuse me?"

Yamaguchi looked puzzled by Takatsuki's answer.

But then he noticed Nanako, who was carrying a large bag, and he turned his attention to her.

"Miss Katsuragi, are you going somewhere?"

"Ah yes... I'm staying at a friend's house this evening. Professor Takatsuki will be staying in my apartment instead."

"What? Professor Takatsuki, you're going to spend the night in that apartment?"

Surprised, Yamaguchi turned to Takatsuki.

Takatsuki smiled and nodded.

"Yes, with Fukamachi as well! We boys are having a sleepover!"

"No, I told you: It's not a sleepover! ...We're going to confirm whether strange things happen in the apartment when someone other than Miss Katsuragi is there."

At Naoya's explanation, Yamaguchi nodded in understanding.

"What a challenge; is this also a part of your college research? Ghosts and stigmatized properties and so on..."

Yamaguchi was regarding Takatsuki as though he was starting to see him as a bit of a weirdo. Well, when it came to university professors, most people imagined them doing more serious research. Even Naoya had that impression, until he met Takatsuki.

Seemingly unaffected by this, Takatsuki smiled and nodded again.

"Certainly, it's a part of my research… By the way, Mr. Yamaguchi, do you live around here?"

"Huh? Ah yes… Well spotted."

"You were walking in the opposite direction from the station, you see. This is great; is there a supermarket in the area that you recommend? I'm thinking of buying food for tonight."

"I see; in that case, if you continue down this road, there's a place that's cheap and has a good selection…"

"Is that so? Thank you for your help," Takatsuki said to Yamaguchi, a wide smile on his face.

Nanako seemed to recall something as she adjusted her grip on her bag. "Come to think of it, Yamaguchi was a huge help to me once."

"Oh? What happened?"

At Takatsuki's question, Nanako looked a little bashful.

"One night, I heard the scratching sound, and I couldn't take it anymore, so I ran outside. I was afraid to go back to my apartment, so I was thinking about waiting it out at a convenience store until morning, but by chance, Mr. Yamaguchi walked in… I feel guilty about it now, but he let me stay with him."

"I thought it wouldn't be a great idea to invite a young woman to come stay in a messy bachelor pad, but it would be even worse to let her pass the night at the convenience store. But I don't mind you relying on me like that. Really… I regret showing you that apartment now, Miss Katsuragi."

Yamaguchi's expression was ashamed, but those two words warped and distorted.

Naoya frowned.

Which meant he didn't regret it at all. Did he show Nanako that room on purpose, knowing strange things would happen…? Maybe.

Suddenly, Yamaguchi turned his gaze to Naoya and smiled—though, it was more condescending than friendly.

"This must be tough on you as well, helping your professor. Are you afraid of ghosts?"

"...Not particularly. Anyway, I'm thinking there's a chance nothing will happen tonight. Regardless, I think we might find a clue that will give us some idea of what's going on."

"Huh?"

Yamaguchi's eyes widened a bit at Naoya's reply.

"Oh... Really? Why do you think that?"

"I'm not sure. I just have a feeling."

Naoya's answer was dismissive, and Yamaguchi stared at him with an expression that was difficult to read.

Takatsuki put a hand on Naoya's shoulder from behind.

"Fukamachi, you don't think anything will happen tonight? Please don't say an awful thing like that! If something really scary happens in that apartment, I want to experience it! I haven't seen an actual supernatural phenomenon before, you know? That's why I'm looking forward to tonight. If we really do witness something supernatural, I'm even thinking of writing and publishing an academic article about it!"

"Indeed... As expected of a university professor... **That's amazing.**"

Yamaguchi was looking at Takatsuki as though his estimation of the other man was getting stranger and stranger. He clearly didn't think Takatsuki was amazing at all, but even Naoya couldn't really argue with him about that.

After seeing Nanako off at the station, they went to the supermarket Yamaguchi had recommended. It turned out to be very affordable, just as he had said.

They bought boxed meals, prepared side dishes, and some bottles of tea. Naoya also took the opportunity to chastise Takatsuki when he went to browse the snacks, reminding him that they weren't playing around. Afterward, they headed back to Nanako's apartment.

There was nothing for them to do once they finished eating.

Naoya had been told he could do as he liked until something happened, so he took a small paperback from his bag to read. Takatsuki was typing away on his laptop, having set it up on the low surface that served as Nanako's tea table. Despite Takatsuki's cheerful declaration that they were having a sleepover for men or whatever, the reality was unexpectedly quiet.

Before long, Naoya raised his head from his book, having grown tired of reading.

Takatsuki was still looking at his laptop.

"What's wrong? Are you bored?"

Perhaps he noticed Naoya's gaze, because Takatsuki paused his typing and looked over.

Naoya put down his book and sat up straighter.

"Yeah, a little."

"Well, something like this is the same as observing wild animals; you're basically just waiting for something to happen. You don't know when things might get interesting, so you need a surprising amount of patience."

Takatsuki shrugged lightly.

"Speaking of, Fukamachi, I forgot to ask you something."

"What is it?"

"Do you live alone?"

"...Yes."

Naoya nodded.

"I see; that's good," Takatsuki murmured.

"Why is it good?"

"Ah, well, if you lived with your parents, for example, and your mother's delicious cooking or something was waiting for you at home, I'd feel bad. I would have to call your parents to introduce myself, like, 'I'm sorry; my name is Takatsuki, and I'm indebted to your son.'"

"...No, it's fine. You don't have to do that."

"It's not fine! Introductions should be done properly! Fukamachi, where do your parents live?"

Takatsuki's persistent questioning made Naoya go quiet for a moment.

It was normal to ask questions about a person's hometown. Takatsuki probably didn't even mean anything by it.

He couldn't keep his mouth shut forever, so Naoya answered honestly.

"They…live in Yokohama."

"Yokohama? Wait, Fukamachi, you really live alone?"

It was an understandable thing to ask. Seiwa University was in Chiyoda. He could very well commute there from Yokohama.

"I wanted to move out of my parents' house quickly and try living on my own. I talked to my parents about it, and for some reason they agreed, so…"

"Hmm. I see."

Takatsuki nodded.

Does he think it's odd? Naoya wondered, subtly watching Takatsuki's demeanor. He didn't want people to look at him with self-serving pity in their eyes after having come to the incorrect conclusion that there must be trouble in his family home.

But Takatsuki smiled softly.

"I see. Then we're the same," he said.

"The…same?"

"I also started living on my own as soon as I started college. My parents' house and university were both in Tokyo, but just like you, I wanted to move out as soon as I could."

"Really?"

"Yep. Really."

Takatsuki didn't say anything else. He went back to his typing, possibly preparing class materials. So Naoya didn't ask him anything else, either.

But—just a little, he was surprised.

With his ever-present smile and ubiquitous kindness, Takatsuki seemed like the kind of person who had been raised in a loving, happy, comfortable home. For some reason, the fact that Takatsuki had gone to live on his own at a young age didn't match up with Naoya's image of him. Well, maybe it really was just that he had wanted to live alone.

But if Takatsuki wasn't offering that information, Naoya didn't think it was right to ask.

He wasn't allowed to get too involved with others. If he breached their walls, they might do the same to him. He had to protect the barrier between himself and other people.

Let's change the subject, Naoya thought.

"Professor?"

"Hmm, what is it, Fukamachi?"

"...Do you really think there are ghosts at work here?"

"Well...I'm not sure."

Takatsuki kept typing, and the answer he gave was not what Naoya had expected. In front of Yamaguchi, he had said how much he hoped ghosts were involved.

Long fingers dancing lightly over his keyboard, Takatsuki elaborated.

"You know, Fukamachi, the unexplained is made up of two things: phenomenon and interpretation."

"Phenomenon and interpretation?"

"Yes. For example, Fukamachi, what do you think thunder is?"

The conversation suddenly veered off course.

"Does it matter what I think it is...? Thunder is thunder. Deep, loud booming sounds, followed by flashes of lightning... It's a natural phenomenon."

"That's right. Actually, people are still researching the principles behind how thunder is generated. There are various theories. We don't fully understand it even in the modern era, so for people living in the past, it was a totally incomprehensible and terrifying phenomenon. They absolutely could not conceptualize it was merely a natural occurrence. That's why people in olden times came up with the idea of the Thunder God. They *interpreted* the *phenomenon* known as thunder as the noise that reverberated to the earth when a demon who lived in the heavens played the big round drum that he carried on his back. When lightning struck the Imperial Palace in the Heian period, they believed that the exiled Sugawara no Michizane had transformed into a Thunder God and was exerting his wrath upon them. If it wasn't for that interpretation, they would have just seen it as lightning striking, rather than divine punishment... In other words, it's usually the human mind that turns specters into specters and gives birth to monsters."

"But why come up with such frightening interpretations? Wouldn't it be better to just think of something as a phenomenon, rather than create gods and monsters for it?"

"Because it's more frightening to let a phenomenon go unexplained. People fear situations they can't put a cause to," Takatsuki answered.

"Religion is a good example. Why do we die? What happens after death? What are we before we're born? Giving an explanation to things like that, things we don't really understand, so that people can have peace of mind, is one of the functions of religion. It's the same with other phenomena. Rather than leaving thunder as something we are afraid of because we don't understand it, interpreting it as 'something caused by the gods in the heavens' gives us some relief. Because if something is the work of spirits, we may be able to avoid it. People don't want to accept the things that scare them as they are, so they create a mythos around those things. We try to define the world through interpretation so that we can put it into terms we can understand. Even if what we come up with is a bit unrealistic, it's better than having no explanation at all."

"Is that so...? Or is that your 'interpretation' of things, Professor?"

"Mm, well, that may be. A scholar's job is to interpret."

A small laugh slipped out of Takatsuki before he continued talking.

"But I think it's a pretty common view that people are afraid of what they can't explain... Fukamachi, have you ever seen the horror movie *Ring*?"

Now he was bringing up movies?

Conversation with Takatsuki skipped and jumped all over the place. His lectures were the same, freewheeling between Buddhist tales from the Kamakura period to articles in contemporary weekly magazines. Perhaps the vast amount of knowledge stored in Takatsuki's head was all equally managed within him, and there were proper connections between everything.

"...Um, that's the one where Sadako comes out of the well, right? I've seen the first movie."

"Yes. That one was remade in Hollywood. Have you seen the remake?"

"Ah, no, just the Japanese one."

"I see. If you have the chance, I think you should watch them both and compare. You can clearly see the different approaches that Japan and America take toward horror. It's quite interesting from a cross-cultural point of view... When people who have watched both versions are asked which one they found scarier, most of them choose the Japanese version."

"Is that because of the script or the cinematography?"

"I'm sure the cinematography has something to do with it. The lighting and colors are completely different. The American movie doesn't have the slimy, pale tones that the Japanese one does. But Hollywood films have larger special effects budgets, so the visuals can get pretty scary... Nevertheless, the Japanese movie is more frightening. I think the reason lies in the plot."

Takatsuki was speaking like he did during lectures. When he wasn't acting like a child, he really was a teacher and a researcher to the core.

He's a bit of an enigma, Naoya mused. The youthfully cheerful man with no common sense—and the presently calm academic. Which one was the real Takatsuki?

The professor continued his commentary in his gentle, pleasant voice.

"Hollywood's *The Ring* is very thorough. It paints a precise picture of Samara's—the American version's Sadako's—background. Consequently, the capacity for tragedy is really high, I believe. You even come to feel sympathetic toward Samara. But in Japan's *Ring*, you only have a vague idea of what kind of person Sadako is, which is exactly what makes her more terrifying... Though, I think there are plenty of other reasons why, depending on the viewer, they might find Samara less scary. Like how after she comes out of the television, her movements are very clipped."

With both hands, Takatsuki showed what he meant by clipped movements. Naoya laughed despite himself.

Takatsuki looked at him again and kept speaking.

"The things we don't understand are scary. That's why people try to justify them, interpret them... What's important, Fukamachi, is *how* we interpret phenomena. We must be careful when we interpret things, because a poor interpretation can distort the phenomenon itself."

"Distort...?"

"For example, the 'encountering a long-haired woman in white standing in the dark on your way home' phenomenon. Some people interpret that as a ghost story. But in reality, it was just a living person—a woman with long hair wearing white clothes. In this case, the phenomenon was distorted by the interpretation. A living person was swapped out for a ghost, and the story transforms into a fable."

The person who interpreted that story probably didn't consider it a lie. Until he found out the woman was alive, in his eyes, that situation had been a ghost encounter.

But that wasn't reality.

Interpretation could alter reality—distort the truth.

"And there's one more thing we have to be careful of."

Takatsuki's hand closed his laptop with a snap.

Suddenly lifting his gaze, he stared fixedly at the wall.

The wall separating Nanako's apartment from the one next door.

"There are people in this world who will deliberately disguise phenomena to incite incorrect interpretations. That is the current offense here: lying to deceive someone."

Naoya nearly reacted at the word *lying*.

He played it off by following Takatsuki's gaze to the wall. The wall where knocking was said to be heard was currently silent. There were no signs of activity.

But Takatsuki's eyes were boring into the wall as if he could see straight through it.

"Going back to this case, the present phenomena are: hearing sounds at night from an apartment that should be unoccupied, a handprint being left on the door of a second-floor balcony, and finding hair in the apartment that doesn't belong to the occupant. Miss Katsuragi's interpretation of these events is 'supernatural activity,' and certainly this situation does seem to point in that direction. However, ghosts aren't the only things capable of creating these phenomena."

Oh, could it be…? Naoya thought, listening to his professor speak. Perhaps Takatsuki had figured it out ages ago.

About the reality, rather than the interpretation, of what was happening in this apartment.

"Professor. Um…"

Naoya was about to say something, but—

A furious bang, like something slamming into the balcony door, interrupted him.

Startled, Naoya whipped his head around to look. With the curtains over the balcony door drawn closed, he couldn't see a thing.

Almost in sync, Naoya and Takatsuki stood and approached the balcony door.

Takatsuki flung open the curtains.

"…!"

For a second, Naoya's breath caught.

There was a handprint on the glass door, left there in a viscous deep-red liquid that looked just like blood.

The balcony was empty, unchanged from how it had appeared in the afternoon.

Despite that, ignoring the way the scarlet handprint had started to drip down the glass, Naoya opened the door and stepped out onto the balcony.

Without pausing, he reached out to touch the partition separating Nanako's balcony from the one next door.

As I thought. The partition should have been fixed in place, but he could move it easily.

At the same time, there were signs of someone moving around on the neighboring balcony. The sound of panicked footsteps rushing back inside the unoccupied apartment and the closing of a glass door.

This wasn't the work of ghosts.

A human was doing this.

"Wait!"

Forcing his way onto the other balcony, Naoya chased after the flee-ing perpetrator. The apartment was pitch-black without any lights on, but he could just make out the culprit trying to open the front door. Not good. At this rate, they might get away.

Getting the door open, the perpetrator flew out of the apartment.

Immediately, there was a bellow—"*Move!*"—from what could only be the culprit's voice.

Naoya froze. *No way*, he thought. No way had Takatsuki left Nana-ko's apartment to lie in wait for the criminal. No, that was beyond reckless. There was no way a guy who looked like a well-bred little gen-tleman could apprehend someone.

Frantic, Naoya rushed out the front entrance, and—

With a great *thud*, the floor of the corridor shook.

Oh no, he thought, awash with dread as he looked at the face of the man who was stretched out on the floor.

But—Naoya's eyes widened in surprise.

It wasn't Takatsuki lying there.

A solid frame. A friendly face.

It was Yamaguchi, the real estate agent.

Standing opposite him, fixing his jacket collar and smiling, was Takatsuki.

"P-Professor…? Wh-what did you…?"

"I think it's called a shoulder throw?"

"A shoulder throw…"

"It's a self-defense technique that KenKen taught me! I'm stronger than I look, you know!"

Takatsuki puffed out his chest with a little *ahem*.

Naoya wanted to ask who "KenKen" was, but someone who appeared to be a first-floor resident had come up the stairs to see what the fuss was, so he held back.

They asked the resident to call the police after explaining the situation. While they waited, they checked on Yamaguchi. He didn't seem unconscious, but having landed on his back, it seemed likely he wouldn't be able to move much for a while.

"Why would a realtor scare someone who rents from their company...?"

Naoya looked down at Yamaguchi in disgust. The other man was scowling from pain and refused to meet his eyes. Well, the police would figure out the details anyhow.

Gazing at Yamaguchi from above, just like Naoya, Takatsuki spoke.

"In large part, I think it's because he was interested in Miss Katsuragi, no?"

"Huh?"

Naoya looked at Takatsuki with confusion. He didn't understand why someone would purposefully frighten someone they like. This wasn't like an elementary school kid bullying their crush.

"Well, he lives around here, doesn't he? Miss Katsuragi said he helped protect her when she ran to a convenience store in the middle of the night, right? I thought that sounded like too much of a coincidence."

"Ah... Then did you suspect this was all his doing at that point?"

Thinking back to Takatsuki's behavior during the day, it seemed likely he had been making all that fuss about ghosts on purpose. Although, he did ordinarily get worked up over the supernatural, so it was hard to say whether it was a real reaction or an act, but—in hindsight, it probably was a performance he put on for Yamaguchi's sake.

"It wasn't then; it was earlier than that. It was when he got upset after I pointed out the scratch marks on the wall, to be precise."

Yamaguchi looked openly shocked at Takatsuki's words.

Takatsuki stared down at him with a slight sneer.

"You didn't mean to scratch the wall, did you? You're a realtor; you wouldn't want to damage your product. So you were careful, but... You put something over the wall, like paper, and scratched on top of that, right? That's why the wallpaper wasn't damaged even though the sounds Miss Katsuragi heard were quite loud. But you scratched a little too hard and left faint marks behind... As for people who would be able to go into apartments that are usually locked and hit or scratch the walls, it's really only landlords and real estate agents. That's why I suspected Yamaguchi. And when we went to the real estate agency earlier, we saw a woman there with long hair. I think he found one of her hairs that had fallen on the floor and planted it in Miss Katsuragi's apartment. He also had access to the key to her apartment and could come and go from the balcony as well."

Come to think of it, outside Nanako's balcony was the neighboring house's cherry tree. After dark it would have been possible for someone to come and go from the balcony without being noticed, because the tree would camouflage them.

"Speaking of, Professor, what about the red handprint from earlier? How do you think that was done?"

Both of Yamaguchi's hands were clean. Naoya figured he would have had to put ink or something on his hands to leave such a deep-red print.

"He probably put wet ink on a piece of paper beforehand and slammed it against the glass door. That's what I would have done. It takes extra time to remove gloves, and if you're not careful taking them off, you could get ink on your hands and clothes. I suspect if we searched the road beneath the balcony thoroughly, we would find the paper evidence. Although it could have been blown away by the wind."

Yamaguchi was avoiding their gazes again, looking guiltier by the second. It seemed Takatsuki's theories were spot-on.

"Actually, he probably intended to hide in the apartment next door for a while after placing the handprint. But since you fearlessly charged onto the other balcony, Fukamachi, he panicked and ran... Say, why were you convinced we weren't dealing with a ghost?"

"I just...had a feeling."

"A feeling? But you suspected Yamaguchi from the beginning, didn't you?"

It was Naoya's turn to stare at Takatsuki in surprise.

Stooping down a little to peer closely at Naoya's face, Takatsuki elaborated.

"It was around the time Yamaguchi showed us the neighboring apartment, I think. The way you looked at him was odd, somehow, and you would scowl at him here and there... So what was it that made you suspicious of him, hmm?"

He was too close. Takatsuki's sense of other people's personal space was fundamentally off, Naoya thought.

But for some reason, he couldn't avert his gaze from Takatsuki's.

His eyes looked once more like they had been dyed indigo. Naoya could see the night sky in them, the one that made him feel like it would swallow him whole. That impossibly deep, enticing blue.

Those eyes—he couldn't tear his own away from them.

"Hey, Fukamachi—could you answer me?"

"It's because...he was lying then."

Before he even processed what was happening, Naoya was very obediently offering up those words to Takatsuki.

Then, with a single blink, the color of the night sky disappeared from Takatsuki's eyes, and Naoya came to his senses.

He had a feeling he had just said something he shouldn't have.

If Takatsuki asked him how he knew Yamaguchi was lying, he'd be done for. This was bad.

"Ah, um, I like to observe people, as a hobby! If I pay attention to someone's behavior and mannerisms, I can somehow tell if they're lying. I can't really explain how, but...I've been able to do it quite a bit."

Naoya lined up explanations as a defense before anyone could ask him more questions.

He wasn't sure if he would be able to trick Takatsuki, who himself had proven to be a skilled observer of others. Naoya hadn't realized his own behavior had been under such scrutiny earlier in the day.

"I see. People watching, huh? You really do seem to have a keen eye. To be able to discern when others are lying—I think that's amazing."

As he spoke, Takatsuki finally stood back up away from Naoya's face. Looking down from his usual height, he smiled.

"Ah, I'm glad you assisted me with this one! You're sensible, you can read maps, your observation skills are excellent, and on top of all that, you've got guts! I was able to catch Yamaguchi in the corridor because you rushed after him on the balcony. Outstanding work, Fukamachi."

At that moment, they heard police cars in the distance. The downstairs resident must have called the police as they had asked.

As soon as they heard the sirens, Yamaguchi hastily tried to get up from his position sprawled out on the door. But Takatsuki was on him in a heartbeat, using his strong knee to press Yamaguchi's shoulder back down.

"Mr. Yamaguchi, please remain where you are until the police arrive. Keep quiet, don't try to get up, and don't make a break for it. Understood?"

"Y-yes..."

In response to the professor's pleasant smile and chilling tone, Yamaguchi went back to lying down.

He really is an enigma, Naoya thought, watching Takatsuki's contrasting mannerisms. He couldn't tell if the man was a simpleminded child or a coolheaded adult.

A few days after that incident, Naoya was once again summoned to Takatsuki's office.

When he had agreed to help with the case, he had given Takatsuki his cell number for contact purposes, which turned out to be a mistake. The professor called him, his tone totally carefree, and asked, "Can you come to my office after class?"

When he got to the office, Naoya was filled in on the details of what happened in Nanako Katsuragi's apartment.

After he was taken away by police, Yamaguchi confessed frankly to the crime.

Just as Takatsuki had said, Yamaguchi had taken a liking to Nanako when she came looking for an apartment, and he purposefully recommended a unit with an unoccupied apartment next door. After she had settled into the place, he apparently sneaked in and out of the empty unit, pretending to be a ghost. He thought that if he could frighten her that way, then swoop in as her savior at the exact right moment, then maybe he would have a chance with her.

"...I—I don't understand *why* he thought he could win over a woman like that..."

Naoya muttered his frustrations, and Takatsuki laughed.

"Well, it might have gone well, you know? Miss Katsuragi didn't seem to bear any ill feelings for Mr. Yamaguchi when he offered her protection at that convenience store in the middle of the night. People who have been pushed to their limits are vulnerable to a helping hand."

"He's disgusting, truly."

"I agree with you there. His behavior was extremely ungentlemanly and despicable."

If she hadn't reached out to Takatsuki, would Nanako have eventually ended up dating Yamaguchi? Without her ever realizing that everything was Yamaguchi's doing? It was awful to think about.

As usual, Takatsuki nursed a cup of cocoa—with marshmallows—in one hand as they spoke.

"It seems Miss Katsuragi has decided to move out of that apartment, after all. She found a friend willing to split rent with her, so as soon as they find somewhere new, she's going to move."

"That's probably for the best."

Naoya nodded, holding the Great Buddha cup in his hand.

In the end, she didn't have a ghost—she had a pseudo-stalker of a real estate agent. It was smart for her to avoid living alone until she could regain her peace of mind.

"Ah, but I'm so disappointed! There was no real apparition this time, either! What a shame... I really thought this case would be the one."

Naoya thought he should probably tell Takatsuki that it was ill-advised to air his innermost thoughts.

But it was no longer his job to be Takatsuki's common sense.

He had probably only called Naoya to his office today to tell him what had happened with the case. That was just common courtesy.

Once Naoya finished his coffee, he would get up and leave the office. Then he and Takatsuki would resume their former roles, as the one who stood at the lectern and taught—and the one who sat and listened to those teachings. That level of distance between them was exactly right, Naoya thought. There would be no more Takatsuki invading his personal space to stare into his eyes or serving him a drink like this. It would be farewell to the colorful Buddha, too.

At least, that's what Naoya thought.

"Ah, but look, Fukamachi. I got a new consultation request!"

Takatsuki pulled his laptop close.

He turned the screen, which was open to his email, toward Naoya, who had nearly spit out his coffee.

"I was thinking of going to hear about it right away, but when are you free?"

"Wh-what, me…?"

"I mean, you told me you'd help me part-time, didn't you?"

"And I did! Wasn't it just a one-time thing?"

"I don't remember saying it would only be one time, though."

Takatsuki's expression was puzzled.

Naoya felt dizzy. He thought back and realized Takatsuki hadn't mentioned a time frame when he asked Naoya to assist him. Exactly how long was he planning to employ Naoya for?

"Nonetheless, I only planned to help the one time. And anyway, I want to look for a more normal part-time job, if I'm going to have one. Please ask another student to help you from now on. I'm going home after I finish drinking this."

"What? No! I don't want another student; I want you!"

Naoya almost spat out his coffee again.

"…Are you a child?! Aren't you an associate professor?! Can't you say things more maturely?! There must be so many other, more scholarly expressions you could use!"

"More maturely…? Um, how about, 'Upon considering the capabilities necessary to assist in my research, I have concluded that there is no person more qualified than Fukamachi'?"

"Ugh, never mind, it doesn't matter if you rephrase it if the sentiment is ridiculous to begin with! I'm only going to say this once—there are tons of students who have common sense and can read maps, okay?!"

"But other students can't do things the way you do, right? What I want is your ability to recognize lies."

Naoya was at a loss for words. He shouldn't have said anything about that, after all.

His mug was still about one-third full. He wondered if he should just gulp it all down and leave quickly. But he had a feeling that if Takatsuki said something weird again while he was drinking, he would definitely spit it out this time.

Takatsuki said he wanted Naoya's ability to recognize lies.

How could he calmly say such a thing?

"…Doesn't it…creep you out?"

The question slipped from Naoya's mouth.

"Huh? Why would it?"

Takatsuki's head cocked to the side. He looked just like the dog from that one famous painting with the gramophone.

"Because usually…when I tell people I can hear lies *differently*, they say it's creepy. Or they just don't believe me."

"Whether I believe it or not, I saw you in action. I think your observational skills are incredible."

Takatsuki, as ever, wore a smile.

When it came to observation, Naoya thought Takatsuki's abilities far outstripped his own. In Nanako's case, for example, Takatsuki seemed to see through everything along the way.

But there was no warping in the professor's voice, and Naoya could tell everything he said was sincere.

He genuinely wanted to keep Naoya by his side.

"I don't want to stop working with you. I want you to continue being my assistant."

Takatsuki's voice was soft, pleasant, and perfectly honest.

His smile was like a bright, cloudless sky…

Even though the night sky was hidden behind his eyes.

Suddenly, the urge to bare everything within Naoya's soul to Takatsuki reared up from the depths of his heart.

About that midnight festival—and his ears, too. If he told his professor everything, what kind of expression would the other man have?

Would he say, "What an interesting story," with his eyes sparkling like usual?

Or would he pity Naoya for how rough his life had been?

Or…would he try to solve the mystery, like he had for Nanako?

…*This is stupid; stop it*, Naoya thought, shoving his thoughts back down. He let out a huge sigh.

He couldn't talk about it. He *shouldn't* talk about it.

That would be crossing the line.

The barrier between Takatsuki and himself. A wall bearing a sign that said No ENTRY BEYOND THIS POINT.

But still, if Takatsuki was to step up to the edge of that wall on purpose and reach out a hand to Naoya—well, it would be fine to go along with him then, as long as Naoya stayed within his own walls.

Takatsuki was intriguing enough to follow him to that extent.

"…Okay, I'll do it. I'll work for you."

"Really?"

Takatsuki's eyes lit up again. Seeing his expression, Naoya thought he had no choice.

Takatsuki really did look just like the golden retriever his family used to own. The dog's name was Leo. Takatsuki's face looked just like Leo's used to when they told him it was time to go for a walk. And Naoya was a sucker for that face.

Chapter 2:
The Girl Who Spits Up Needles

University summer break was long.

Two months long, to be precise. There were some students who were spending their break busy with part-time jobs, travel, and training camps, but for students who weren't involved in anything like that, it was a little bit unbearable.

Students like Naoya Fukamachi, for example.

"It's...so...hot..."

Naoya muttered vacantly while lying on the floor of his rental studio apartment in Nishi-Kanda. He flapped a paper fan at himself, trying to cool down.

A huge chorus of cicadas was singing outside. They sang so vigorously it surprised Naoya—and made him wonder at how many cicadas there were, even in Tokyo. The sun blazed relentlessly, scorching the asphalt. Every day the weather forecast contained the phrase "record highs" in spades. Naoya tried to use the air conditioner as little as possible to save on electricity, so he spent his afternoons in the library, but on days this hot, one had to prepare to meet their maker when simply stepping outside. It was days like this that made Naoya think seriously about the gravity of global warming.

It had already been about one month since summer break had begun.

Which meant he had another month of summer heat ahead of him. If he had classes to go to, he could at least summon the will to leave his apartment, because he had no choice. But with nothing to do, he didn't even want to go outside.

Then his smartphone vibrated from where it lay on the floor.

He had a message. It was from someone in the language class group message on LINE.

"*Heeey. Anyone wanna go to the beach? I have a friend working part-time at a beachside club on Enoshima, and he invited me. He could give us a little discount.*"

Language courses were the only college-level classes that shared a similar vibe as the ones taken in high school. Since they were compulsory, there weren't many students who skipped, and the format was similar to high school English classes as well.

Because of that, there was a feeling of camaraderie between classmates. Those in the same language courses hung out a lot more than students who shared other courses. They'd often go out drinking or do things together. That was why the group LINE message had been created.

Naoya stared at the message for a little while and watched as the first replies and emojis started rolling in. "*I'm in!*" "*Sorry, I can't.*" "*Of course I wanna go, but I'm gonna look bad in my swimsuit unless I lose a few more pounds.*"

Naoya quietly sent in his own response amid the frenzy of conversation.

"*Sorry, I'm broke, so I can't go. Send pictures, though. I want to experience the summer memories, too.*"

He had to be careful when declining an invitation.

Refusing too bluntly could cause offense. He could be labeled a bad egg and get shunned for it. The necessary elements for a good refusal were: a light apology, an excuse that made the other party think it couldn't be helped, and a sentiment that made it seem like he *really* wished he didn't have to miss out... As expected, being so calculating made Naoya feel a little disgusted with himself, but he had grown accustomed to doing things that way in his life.

Someone immediately replied to his message with an OK! emoji, and Naoya let out a little sigh when he saw it.

The sea, huh, he thought idly.

He hadn't been to the sea in a long time. All the people in his language classes were nice. They would probably have a great time. Running barefoot toward the water's edge through the scorching sand, screaming in excitement along the way, then plunging into the sea. Eating ramen at the beach house after swimming to their hearts' content. Maybe even splitting watermelons and playing beach volleyball.

Closing his eyes, Naoya thought about how much fun it would all be. *Don't think about it.* Activities like that happened outside of his walls.

In any case, Naoya's plans for the summer amounted to grading problem sets and correcting essays part-time for elementary and middle school students. He had signed on as a subcontractor for a remote-learning cram school, because it was easy to do the work from home or the library. He didn't have plans to go anywhere in particular. It was difficult to travel alone, and he really didn't have a lot of money. He thought it would at least be nice during his break to see a few of the movies that had piqued his interest. He had an excessive amount of time on his hands.

Summer vacation can't end soon enough, Naoya thought.

His smartphone vibrated again.

He planned to ignore it if it was a text, but the phone kept vibrating. Someone was calling him.

He reached for the phone and saw Takatsuki's name displayed on the screen.

For a second, he hesitated—then resigned himself and answered the call. "...Yes, hello?"

"Ah, Fukamachi, hello. It's hot again, isn't it? Would you like to go see ghosts with me?"

The voice coming through the phone was pleasant to listen to.

But the conflicting statements delivered by the voice were an odd match, to say the least.

Naoya hadn't seen Takatsuki since his last lecture before summer break. In the month since then, it seemed like, for better or for worse, the professor hadn't changed at all.

Naoya pressed a hand lightly to his forehead, thinking. Things probably made sense in Takatsuki's head, but an ordinary person like Naoya needed some kind of connection between topics to understand.

"...Um, are you talking about work? Did you get another ghost-related investigation request?"

"No, not work. It's just a normal invitation to go see ghosts. It'll be fun!"

Even though he was a grown adult, his words were childish as usual.

But what did he mean by "going to see ghosts"?

"Wait, Fukamachi, are you at your parents' house for summer vacation, by chance? Or maybe you're in the middle of reveling in your summer break, getting all tanned at the beach or the pool with friends or a girlfriend? If so, I'm sorry! You won't be able to join me, right?"

"I have not gone back to my parents' house, I do not have friends or a girlfriend, and I don't like summer, so no, I have not been 'reveling' in my summer break, nor do I intend to."

"...I'm sorry; I shouldn't have asked any of that, should I?"

Well, it seemed he had enough sense to worry that he may have hurt someone's feelings.

Naoya let out another small sigh and shifted positions. His own body heat had started to warm his spot on the floor, so he moved to another area that was still cool.

"What do you mean 'going to see ghosts?' Like an abandoned ruin? Or sneaking into a dilapidated hospital in the middle of the night as a test of courage? That sounds pretty good, actually; it probably wouldn't be so hot."

"Ah, no, we'd be going during the day, but not to those places. I want to go see ghost scrolls."

"Ghost scrolls?"

"Yes. Paintings of ghosts on scrolls! You can only see them at this time of year!"

On the other end of the phone, Takatsuki's voice bubbled with excitement.

It's nice that he always seems to be having fun, Naoya thought as he lay spread out over the floor.

Takatsuki had invited him to the Yanaka Encho Festival.

Throughout the month of August, at the Zenshoan temple in the Yanaka neighborhood of Tokyo, an exhibition of ghost scrolls collected by a man named Sanyutei Encho was open to the public.

Sanyutei Encho was a *rakugo* storyteller and author who was active from the end of the Edo period to the Meiji period. His representative works included "The Tale of the Peony Lantern" and "The True View at the Kasane Marsh." Naoya read about him at the library after Takatsuki mentioned him, and his plays seemed pretty scary. People tended to think of *rakugo* as a comedic medium, but Encho's specialties had been ghost stories and emotional plays about human nature.

Naoya couldn't go to the sea with everyone, but Takatsuki's invitation did interest him a bit. It seemed like a fun idea to go see the scrolls, since they could only be viewed once a year around this time. And anyway, he didn't really want to be someone who stayed sequestered indoors all summer.

So on a day in late August, Naoya made his way to Nippori Station.

It was his first time going to Nippori, which was a spectacular train station with retail venues inside and tons of people milling about. He was meeting Takatsuki by the north ticket gate. While listening to the music streaming through the earbuds he had jammed into both ears, Naoya reached into his bag for his transit card. He went to swipe it at the ticket gate—and stopped short unintentionally.

Takatsuki was standing by the wall opposite the ticket gate.

Even though it was summer break, he was wearing a suit, as usual. Because he was already quite tall in addition to being dressed that way, he stood out considerably from the people around him, who were out-fitted as one would expect for summertime and showing a lot more skin. But that wasn't what made Naoya pause.

There was another man standing next to Takatsuki.

At first glance, Naoya thought, *He's huge.*

The man was even taller than Takatsuki. On top of that, his body was so well-built that you could tell from miles away. His short-sleeved shirt showed off his solidly muscled arms. Moreover, like some kind of finishing touch, the man was wearing sunglasses. Quite frankly, he was scary.

The frightening man was talking to Takatsuki about something. The professor was smiling as he always did, but no matter how he looked at it, Naoya couldn't help but worry that Takatsuki was being harassed. What should he do? Should he get help?

As Naoya fretted, Takatsuki's gaze landed on him. He beckoned Naoya over with a smile, and seeing no other choice, Naoya reluctantly went through the ticket gate and approached the two men.

"Hi, Fukamachi! I'm glad you came. It's warm today, too, isn't it?"

"...Speak for yourself, Professor, aren't you hot in that? Wearing a suit and a jacket, even."

"Well, I'm a gentleman! And gentlemen wear suits in public. Besides, it's made of lighter fabric, so I don't think it'll get too hot, you know?"

Takatsuki chuckled as he spoke, and sure enough, he didn't seem to be sweating much. Maybe he was someone who didn't mind the heat.

The scary-looking man with the sunglasses didn't speak as he watched the exchange between Naoya and Takatsuki. Was the fact that he hadn't walked away a sign that he was here with Takatsuki? The professor had said some of his graduate students might join them, but this man didn't look anything like a graduate student.

"Ah, I haven't introduced you, have I? Fukamachi, this is KenKen!"

Noticing Naoya's gaze, Takatsuki made the introduction with a bright grin. But there was no way this guy was called KenKen. Had he actually introduced himself that way to Takatsuki? Not a chance.

Then Naoya realized that name—KenKen—sounded familiar.

Oh, right. Wasn't that the person who had taught Takatsuki self-defense? The scary-looking guy opened his mouth.

"...You go to Akira's school?"

He spoke in a low, slightly husky mutter. Naoya hurried to reply.

"I'm a first-year at Seiwa U. My name is Fukamachi."

"...Kenji Sasakura. I'm an old friend of Akira's."

As he talked, the scary-looking man—no, Sasakura—took off his sunglasses.

His face gave the overall impression of sharpness. Both his straight, distinct eyebrows and his slightly almond-shaped eyes turned sharply upward at the outer edge. With or without his shades on, the effect was the same. His facial features weren't bad, but the look in his eyes was too cutting. It was frightening.

Still smiling, Takatsuki gestured to his intimidating friend.

"KenKen lives nearby, and we've been friends since we were little. He just happened to be off work today, so I asked him to come. I know his face is scary, but KenKen isn't a bad person, okay? He's a detective, after all!"

"...Akira. Don't say my face is scary."

"Ah, sorry. Um, then, your presence is scary?"

"That's worse."

Sasakura glared viciously at Takatsuki, who only smiled back without flinching. This was normal for them, it seemed. Naoya really was surprised to hear Sasakura was a detective, though. If anything, he would have said the man looked like he belonged to a more unsavory profession. In any case, Naoya was glad he hadn't alerted the authorities earlier.

Just then, Takatsuki looked over Naoya's shoulder and beckoned in a "come over here" motion. It seemed like someone else who was joining them for the day had just arrived.

"Sorry I'm late!"

A girl wearing a light-blue dress was running toward them, her silky hair swishing back and forth as she moved. She was delicate-looking and quite pretty. She was probably one of the graduate students Takatsuki had invited.

"Ah, you're right on time; it's just that we all got here early. Besides,

Miss Yui isn't here yet. Hirosawa said he couldn't come because he had to fill in last-minute at his part-time job."

"Oh, Yui told me she wouldn't be able to make it today, either! Apparently, the chocolate banana she bought at a local festival stand was bad, and she's got horrible diarrhea."

"That's rough. I'll send her a 'get well soon' email later."

"Oh no, you can't! She told me not to tell you! She said it's embarrassing... I guess I did tell you, though, didn't I? Geez."

"Yep, you sure did. Well then, I'll go with a gentler phrasing. 'I heard you're not feeling well,' or 'How are you doing?' Something like that."

"Yes, something like that! Yui really likes you, Professor. She even told me she would rather die than have diarrhea with you around!"

The girl pressed her hands together as if in prayer while she recounted the conversation. It probably would be quite embarrassing for a girl's favorite teacher to find out she was having tummy troubles.

Then the graduate student turned her gaze to Naoya.

"Huh? Are you the one I met at Professor Akira's office before? Fukamachi, was it? Long time no see!"

Naoya was momentarily confused by her cheerful greeting. He couldn't remember meeting her at all. When had he met someone this pretty?

"Ah, do you not remember me? Maybe because I'm wearing contacts today instead of my glasses. It's me, Ruiko Ubukata. Remember?"

The girl—Ruiko—pointed at her own face.

Frantically scouring his memory, Naoya almost gasped when he remembered.

That's right; he had met her before. The female student who had been sleeping on the floor the first time Naoya was invited to Takatsuki's office. The way she had looked then, with floorboard marks on her cheeks, messy hair, and glasses askew, did not at all match her currently perfectly made-up face.

"Fukamachi, I understand what you're feeling. Miss Ruiko is beautiful, but she usually looks fairly unimpressive..."

"Uh-huh... Women sure are amazing..."

Naoya nodded a little, answering in a small voice. It was like seeing a metamorphosis.

"What I meant to say is: Your memory is amazing, Miss Ubukata. You were half asleep that time and had to leave so quickly; we only met for a moment, but..."

"Ah, I'm not as good as Professor Akira, but I remember people's faces well. I teach part-time at a cram school, so I have to match my students' faces with their names pretty quickly," Ruiko replied.

Apparently, she worked for two cram schools geared toward middle and high school students, and it was essential for her to be able to recognize each student so she could communicate with them.

As everyone who was expected to arrive was present, it was time for the group to get moving.

"On that note, Professor, are you okay with the roads around here? You won't get lost, will you?"

"No, I've been to Yanaka many times, so I'm fine. I remember all the roads... Now then, since we're here, let's cut through Yanaka Cemetery."

In high spirits, Takatsuki headed for the small staircase to the immediate left of the west exit, which led to Yanaka Cemetery.

But Naoya didn't understand why they were purposefully going to walk through a graveyard. Was this a test of courage or something?

Walking at his side, Ruiko noticed Naoya's expression.

"Fukamachi, you're not familiar with Yanaka Cemetery, are you? It's actually a tourist attraction."

"Is that true? Even with the graves?"

"Yep, it's especially popular with foreign tourists. A lot of famous people are buried here. The most famous is the grave of Tokugawa Yoshinobu. Yokoyama Taikan, the artist, is here, too, among others. I mean, even Japanese people go abroad to see the catacombs and visit the graves of famous monarchs and writers and such, right? Don't you think that's pretty much the same thing? Oh, here—bug spray. There are tons of mosquitoes here, so you should put some on."

Ruiko took a small spray bottle out of her bag as she spoke. She was well prepared.

"Thank you, Miss Ubukata."

"Just Ruiko is fine. Actually, call me that, please. Everyone calls me Ruiko."

After Naoya was done, Ruiko passed the bug spray to Takatsuki and Sasakura.

It felt a little cooler inside the cemetery than it had outside of it. Perhaps because of all the trees. Or maybe it was that the thought of a graveyard somehow made people catch a chill. He was told there were famous people buried here, but from Naoya's point of view, as far as the eye could see, there were only regular graves with family names engraved on them.

"By the way, this is a famous haunted spot in Tokyo, so be careful, okay? *Hee-hee.*"

Ruiko laughed mischievously as she and Naoya walked side by side along the path between the headstones.

"Although, all the stories about this place are the same old spooky clichés like seeing a translucent figure walk by or hearing voices, so we can't be sure how much truth there is to them."

"If all the ghost stories are clichéd, does that mean they might not be true?"

"In general, yeah. I mean, stories are things that spread, right? It's quite common for a ghost story told in one place to take root in another, similar place. The Seven School Mysteries are a good example. Anatomical models moving in the middle of the night, the bleeding Mona Lisa, Hanako-san of the toilet, the thirteenth stair, and so on. Every school's Seven Mysteries are similar. Who even knows how many Hanako-sans there are in the whole country, at this point? That's another example of a story that spread to other places, 'school' being the common denominator in that case."

Listening to Ruiko talk was a bit like attending a lecture, as one might expect from a graduate student. Her lively voice and crisp enunciation were lovely to hear.

"What kind of research are you doing, Miss Ruiko?" Naoya asked.

"My research centers on classifying urban legends and rumors. Rather than their contents, I categorize stories based on how and when they appeared. That's why I read a lot of stories online. Relatively recent creations frequently come from internet forums and Twitter."

"Creations... In other words, made-up stories?"

"Right. Untrue stories that someone came up with."

The word *untrue* made Naoya scowl automatically, and he tilted his head to the side in thought.

"If something is a lie, can it still be a research topic?"

"Absolutely! Lies can be quite interesting. I mean, that famous photograph of Nessie was fake, right?"

"Yeah, um, the 'surgeon's photograph,' right?"

Nessie was probably the most famous UMA (unidentified mysterious animal) there was. A plesiosaur-like creature spotted in Loch Ness in the United Kingdom. There had been many sightings of her, among the most well-known being the so-called surgeon's photograph, which was later proved to be a fake. That news had probably been disappointing to the whole world.

"The photo was fake, but because it became famous, the entire world believed in the Loch Ness Monster. A simple lie becoming such a huge story, that alone makes it an indisputable legend, worthy of study. Plus, we can't deny the possibility that any legend started out as nothing more than a hoax."

Ruiko continued.

"I think when you encounter a fake story, you have to think about why it was created and why it spread. It could have just been a joke, or in modern times, a story that got a lot of likes on social media. It could be that someone just wanted to share the story they wrote with others. But if a story doesn't have what it takes to go viral, it won't spread that far. The reasons behind that and the prerequisites for it, that's key... That's the core of my research. What do you think? Interesting, right?"

She grinned at Naoya, one corner of her mouth lifting.

Ruiko looked a lot like Takatsuki then, with her eyes sparkling as she talked animatedly about her interests. She was still something of a budding scholar, but Ruiko would surely someday become a true academic after continuing to follow the path of her research.

"...What you're studying certainly is interesting."

"Right? Hey, Fukamachi, you're also majoring in folklore, right? Are there any topics you're interested in researching?"

"Oh, um, no, I haven't chosen a major yet."

"Really? I thought you must be aiming to join Professor Akira's research seminar since you're so attached to him."

"I'm not attached! Professor Takatsuki got attached to me!"

"...That sounds a little fishy, y'know?"

"It does not! And what do you mean by that anyway?!"

"Heh-heh-heh, so suspicious! Hey, Professor Akira, what's the real truth here?"

With a delighted laugh, Ruiko started talking to the professor. Takatsuki looked back at her, puzzled, then matched pace with her so they were walking side by side. Naoya overheard their conversation as it turned to Ruiko's research, and he was somehow overcome with a sense of relief. Sometimes he really didn't understand what women were thinking.

Feeling an unexpected gaze on himself, Naoya lifted his head to find Sasakura staring down at him.

Sasakura had been walking alongside Takatsuki until a moment ago, but he had switched places with Ruiko since she had gone to monopolize the professor.

Sasakura spoke.

"Hey, kid."

"...It's Fukamachi."

"Fukamachi. Are you into that stuff, too? Urban legends and ghosts and monsters and whatever?"

He might have been trying to communicate normally with Naoya in his own way, but since his voice was so intimidating, Naoya felt like he was being interrogated.

"Not really. I do think Professor Takatsuki's class is interesting, though."

Sasakura scowled at his response. Yikes. His stare was really intense.

"...You know, you don't have to be so scared. I'm not trying to glare at you; my face is just like this."

"That must be difficult."

"I don't need you to pity me over it."

Now he really did seem mad.

Behind them, Ruiko and Takatsuki were chatting excitedly. If he didn't know better, Naoya would say they might seem like a good-looking couple on a date. But listening closely, he could hear them talking about urban legends like the wriggling *kunekune* and the cursed child-stealing puzzle box, the *kotoribako*. Well, if they were enjoying themselves, it was fine.

Suddenly, Sasakura turned right down the path between the graves.

Wondering what was happening, Naoya followed him as he made a left turn soon after. Sasakura was now walking down a path parallel to the one they had started on, one row of graves over.

Wondering if something had been blocking the first path, Naoya turned to look.

He immediately understood.

On the original path, some ways ahead, several crows had gathered. The crows were pecking at the ground with their large black beaks, perhaps looking for dropped food.

They had changed lanes for Takatsuki's sake.

He was afraid of birds.

"...Has Professor Takatsuki been afraid of them since he was young?"

Naoya directed his question at Sasakura.

The other man scowled at Naoya again.

Naoya met his stare, trying with all his might not to flinch. Sasakura let out a sigh.

"...Just so you know. Akira isn't good with birds."

"On campus, once, I saw him almost faint when a dove flew by."

"...He wasn't like that when he was a kid. He even had a pet sparrow in elementary school. The fear came on later."

Sasakura's voice was low enough that the pair behind them wouldn't overhear.

"Does that mean something made him like this?"

"Why do you want to know?"

Surprised by the rebuttal, Naoya snapped his mouth shut.

Sasakura looked down at him with his sharp gaze.

"You're old enough to know there are some things in this world you can ask about out of simple curiosity, and some things you can't, right? What I'm saying is: Drop it. It's not a fun story to hear."

His voice was quiet, but the division it was drawing was clear.

It was the same type of line Naoya often drew. The wall that said "No entry beyond this point." He was being told not to pry into personal matters.

Sasakura's voice struck like a wooden sword. Direct and solid but subdued enough not to cut like a metal blade. Listening to him speak, Naoya thought he must really care about Takatsuki. At that moment, Sasakura was poised to protect his friend.

But then, with a huff, the tone of his voice changed.

"...Although, Akira seems to have really taken a liking to you."

A wry smile combined with an exasperated tone made Sasakura sound just like an elder brother looking out for his much younger sibling. Even though he was probably the same age as Takatsuki.

"For the time being, he's going to keep spending time around you. That means he might actually collapse in front of you someday. So take this, just in case."

Sasakura took out a business card and handed it to Naoya. Seeing that it said TOKYO METROPOLITAN POLICE DEPARTMENT on it, Naoya was taken aback. And CRIMINAL AFFAIRS DEPARTMENT—1ST INVESTIGATIVE DIVISION, no less. This man was like the kind of police officer only seen in TV dramas.

"My cell number is written on the back."

Sure enough, when Naoya flipped over the card, a phone number had been handwritten on the other side.

"If something bad happens, call me. Doesn't matter what time."

"Something bad…?"

"If Akira collapses, you won't be able to carry him alone, right? Besides, you probably know this since you've been around him a bit, but on top of his interests being fundamentally dangerous, his way of thinking is a little weird, too. In a situation where a normal guy would give up, there's a possibility he would just rush in wildly without batting an eye."

Sasakura continued.

"If you're thinking of cutting ties with him, do it sooner rather than later. That's in your best interest. But if you want to stick close to him for a while longer… If anything happens, call me. Got it?"

"Yes… Understood."

Something occurred to Naoya as he stared at the handwritten phone number.

He remembered what Takatsuki had told him before: "…There have been lots of kind people in my life."

Surely, one of the people he had been talking about was Sasakura.

He looked scary, but he was actually a nice person. So nice that he wasn't just looking after Takatsuki—he was looking after Naoya as well.

After continuing for a while, they came to a large road.

Although, it was still bordered on both sides by the graveyard. The cemetery was considerably vast, it seemed. There was a signpost stating that graves of famous people could be found in this section. As Ruiko had said, there were people who had simply come to visit gravestones as one normally did, but they also passed quite a few people who looked like foreign tourists. Japanese cemeteries were probably a novelty to them. They walked about, looking in all directions, guidebooks and cameras in hand. Although, perhaps Naoya's group wasn't that different from the tourists, since it wasn't like they had come to visit a grave, either.

After coming out of Yanaka Cemetery and merging back onto a normal street, they didn't have to go much farther to reach Zenshoan. At the gate, a sign advertising the ghost scroll exhibition stood.

Zenshoan was built by Yamaoka Tesshu during the Meiji period to memorialize those who died in the national conflicts of the Meiji Restoration. However, the building itself was fairly modern, probably because it had been recently rebuilt.

The group took off their shoes, stepped onto the cool wooden floor, and entered the exhibition room, where the ghost scrolls were lined up, hanging side by side. Many of the pieces were by artists so famous even Naoya had heard of them: ones like Tsukioka Yoshitoshi, Maruyama Ōkyo, and Kawanabe Kyōsai. There were a lot of attendees at the exhibition, since the collection could only be seen in the present time of year.

Even though they were called "ghost" scrolls, each artist had their own way of imagining the subject matter. Some of the scrolls were utterly terrifying, while others contained nothing more than a woman wearing a white kimono. There was even an optical illusion of a painting that Naoya thought only showed the moon, clouds, and willow trees, but when he looked at it from farther away, those elements made up the face of a ghost.

"…There's a lot of variation in these, isn't there?"

Naoya spoke in a low voice, and Takatsuki, who was standing next to him, nodded.

"The man who collected these, Sanyutei Encho, hosted storytelling rituals in his lifetime. It's said that in connection with the one hundred stories ritual, he began a collection of one hundred ghost scrolls. Although, if you look into it later, you can see it looks like there are paintings mixed in with his collection that there's no way Encho could have acquired himself."

"Everyone likes scary stories and ghosts and such, don't they? There are a lot of supernatural-themed TV specials in the summer, too…"

"Generally speaking, during extended periods of peace when a culture matures, ghost stories flourish. That was true in the Edo period, and it's true now. We're talking ghost stories for mere entertainment, not those told for moral or religious reasons."

"Ghost stories are popular when things are peaceful?"

"It's strange, isn't it? I think it's probably because, in times of war like the Sengoku period, when corpses were everywhere you looked, death couldn't just be a fantasy."

"A fantasy?"

"I mean, I don't think any of the artists who painted these actually saw ghosts, right? These images are all products of the imagination."

Come to think of it, that had to be the case. There may have been artists who did see actual ghosts, but most of these ghost scrolls depicted things the painters thought up. They weren't real.

"And yet the reason we all look at these paintings of fake ghosts and think *That's a picture of a ghost* is because there's a shared understanding of what ghosts are. Most people have never seen a ghost but still have an image of what one looks like in their heads. The artists who painted these scrolls created images characteristic of their own imaginations within them."

Naoya looked at all the hanging scrolls lined up along the walls of the exhibition room.

A number of ghosts, some resentful, some wearing a smile, some expressionless, all haunting the white spaces of their paintings.

All of them born from the minds of artists who lived long ago.

But even modern humans recognized them as spirits and specters. Even without ever seeing a ghost, everyone understood: This is what ghosts look like.

"I like this painting. She's very beautiful, and there's a tinge of sexuality to her, but there's also a loneliness in her that's very ghostlike, in my opinion. If I ever meet a ghost, I hope it's one like this."

Takatsuki pointed at a painting titled *Ghost in front of the mosquito net* by Hirezaki Eiho.

It was a picture of a woman in a white kimono standing before a mosquito net that was illuminated by a standing paper lantern. Her bound hair had come slightly loose, her downturned face was pale and beautiful, and she was gazing sidelong toward the viewer. It wasn't a frightening painting, and Naoya had a feeling he might not have been able to tell it was a picture of a ghost if he hadn't been told, but—just as Takatsuki said, it really was quite a lonely image.

"Do you think ghosts ever feel lonely?"

"If you had to remain in this world as a ghost, that would be a very lonely experience, don't you think? You'd become something that isn't the same as the living."

Takatsuki continued, elaborating.

"The dead and the living are separate entities. Their existences don't mesh. Say, for example, you became a different creature from someone you loved—I think that would be quite sad—and lonely."

For some reason, as he spoke, Takatsuki's expression became just as lonely as that of the ghost in the painting he was staring at.

A phobia of birds, an excellent memory—the reason he wanted to move out of his parents' home as soon as possible.

Takatsuki being who he was, he probably carried some complex burdens within.

But if he wasn't going to say anything more, Naoya had no intention of crossing that line himself.

He didn't even need to be told by Sasakura. Naoya wasn't the type to pry like that.

"Well, why don't we go look at those next? The paintings on that side are interesting, too."

Takatsuki's eyes were tinged with the color of the night sky as he looked at Naoya, who thought he made the right choice deciding not to ask anything more.

After the exhibition, they decided to walk to the Yanaka Ginza shopping district and have some tea.

Once again, it was Naoya's first time in the area. He had a feeling he had seen the so-called Sunset Staircase, the entrance to the district, on television before. The shopping district had a retro feel, but it was a bit surreal to see a Turkish restaurant lit by multicolored lamps upon first setting foot past the entrance. Perhaps because the area was associated with cats, there were shops here and there selling cat-themed goods, and some places even had cat statues on their roofs.

They bought cake donuts in the shape of cat tails and had decided to keep strolling a bit as they ate when a voice called out to them.

"Ah, Professor Takatsuki!"

The voice came from behind.

When they turned, there were two girls standing a little ways away. One of them was tall, with a slightly bold-looking face and long black hair tied up in a ponytail. The other was a petite, slightly plump, mild-mannered-looking girl with brown hair cut in a short bob.

"Ah, you two are in Folklore Studies II!"

As expected, Takatsuki remembered the faces of every student taking his class and waved at the two girls.

The two of them rushed over with happy expressions.

"I can't believe it—running into Professor Takatsuki in a place like this; it's like a dream!"

"We just went to see the ghost scrolls at a place over there called Zenshoan!"

Takatsuki smiled and nodded.

"Is that so? We just came from there as well. Did you find the scrolls interesting?"

"Yes! Some of them were pretty scary, and it felt like going to a haunted house!"

"The scene Seiu Ito drew from *The Ghost of Chibusa Enoki* was so scary I feel like I'm going to have nightmares about it..."

The girls took turns telling Takatsuki about the experience. The professor was really popular with women. They both seemed genuinely happy to run into Takatsuki, even if it was only by chance.

Then, just as Naoya was thinking that the bold-looking girl's expression had suddenly turned serious, she spoke again. "Professor, I'm sorry, but I think it might have been some sort of fate for us to meet here, because, actually... There's something I want to ask you about."

"Hmm? What is it?"

Takatsuki's face was kind as he prompted her to continue.

"Um... You're investigating strange incidents and the like, right? I saw something like that written on your website."

"A-Aya! Professor Takatsuki is out with his friends right now; we shouldn't bother him!"

The mild-mannered-looking girl gestured to Sasakura and Ruiko. Apparently, Naoya didn't register in her field of vision. Was he so plain that he faded into the background?

But the girl called Aya shook her head with a determined look.

"Kotoko, you say that, but I don't know when I'll see Professor Takatsuki next! If things go on like this until the end of summer break, I'll go crazy!"

The fact that she saw Takatsuki's website and got the idea to consult him meant she was experiencing some kind of mysterious phenomenon. There was a sense of urgency in her voice, just as there had been in Nanako's when they dealt with her case before.

It was a bit thoughtless to interrupt someone's private free time to approach them for help. But it was possible that what she was going through was so frightening that she had no choice.

The girl named Kotoko glanced at Takatsuki with a troubled expression.

"B-but, well, why not just make an appointment for now and meet another day...? We don't want to be rude..."

Her voice was shy.

Takatsuki looked between the two of them before nodding once.

"It seems like something is really bothering you, yes? If that's the case, I'd rather you tell me about it right away."

Somehow managing to find enough seats for the whole group in a café at the end of Yanaka Ginza, they decided to settle in there to listen to the girls' story.

Naoya thought, as Takatsuki's assistant, that he would be the only extra person in attendance, but Ruiko and Sasakura tagged along as well. Ruiko seemed interested in the girls' story, while Sasakura just seemed to have time to waste. The girls—aside from Ruiko—looked a bit reluctant to sit with the very intimidating Sasakura, but nevertheless, they started to open up by the time their orders arrived.

The strong-willed girl's name was Ayane Harasawa, and the shy one was Kotoko Makimura. The two had been friends since middle school and seemed remarkably close. They were both first-years in the Literature Department, but they were in different language classes than Naoya, so he wasn't acquainted with them.

The one having trouble was Ayane.

"Um, Professor, before, you gave us extra credit if we wrote about a weird experience on our report, right? Do you remember what I wrote on that assignment?"

She was talking about the report that got Naoya caught up in Takatsuki's work to begin with.

Taking a sip of his iced tea, which was loaded with sweetener, Takatsuki nodded.

"I remember. You included a photo as well, didn't you? Right, it was like this."

He suddenly looked off into the air.

"*Last week, I went to the large stage at Hibiya Park Concert Hall with friends to hear a performance, and on the way home, I took a little walk in Hibiya Park. I thought, since it was nighttime and quite dark, it would be like a test of courage and might be fun.*

"*Then I found a straw doll on one of the trees in the park. There were tons of needles stuck into it, giving me the strong impression that it was used to curse someone, and I was afraid of it. I took a picture of it just in case, so please take a look. (And thank you for the extra points!)*"

Ayane and Kotoko were astounded.

"...Wow, that's amazing! Professor, you memorized what I wrote?!"

"Yep, my memory is rather good. I remember the photo, too. There were twenty pins, ten ordinary needles, and one nail stuck into the body and head. The doll itself was quite well-made, so I didn't get the feeling it was something crafted out of resentment by an amateur. I thought they might have bought it online or something."

In modern times, where anything could be ordered from the internet with the click of a button, it seemed even cursed items could be easily acquired. Whether that was a good thing, well, it was hard to say.

"So has something happened related to your report?"

"Ah, well… Um, I don't know if you'll believe me, but…ever since I saw that straw doll…needles have…"

"Needles?"

"Needles have been falling, all over…"

Ayane explained the situation.

She told them that, for example, sometimes when she stood up after sitting, pins would fall from the hem of her skirt to the floor with a tinkling sound.

Or if she looked around after getting up, dozens of sewing needles would be strewn over her chair.

When she was walking, she would suddenly see a flash of silver light over her feet—an embroidery needle falling.

The type and number varied by occasion, but before she knew it, needles were falling randomly from all over and around her body.

She told them it had happened countless times.

"That *is* scary. Have you been injured by them at all?"

"I haven't, but… They really are just falling, but somehow, it freaks me out. It's like the needles are haunting me."

Ayane wrapped her arms around herself as she spoke.

At her side, Kotoko began to speak in a trembling voice.

"Um, the friend Aya mentioned in her report was me. I saw the doll, too. When Aya told me she was going to take a picture of it, I asked her to stop. But she said she was going to write about it for her report and didn't listen to me…"

Takatsuki cast his eyes downward and lightly combed through his own hair with one hand. Then he lifted his gaze and looked between Ayane and Kotoko for a little while.

"Miss Makimura, you saw the doll as well, yes? Have needles been falling from your body, too?"

"As for me, no... Nothing strange has been happening to me."

Kotoko shook her head, underscoring her reply.

Takatsuki's head cocked to the side.

"That's odd. You were together when you saw the doll, so why is Miss Makimura unaffected, I wonder? The only thing that separates you is... that Miss Harasawa took a picture and wrote about it in her report, I guess?"

"So that is the cause, then?!"

Ayane's face was scrunched up like she was about to cry. She put her elbows on the table and held her head in her hands.

"I thought that picture was interesting at first, so I set it as my phone background, but then it started to creep me out, so I deleted it. The needles, too—I throw them away as soon as they appear. But I'm telling the truth! Professor, do you believe me? I don't know what to do anymore...!"

"...It's all right; I believe you."

Takatsuki's voice was soft.

Ayane raised her head to look at him, and Takatsuki smiled kindly in return.

"Of course I believe you. It's me we're talking about here."

"Professor Takatsuki..."

Ayane looked at Takatsuki, relief and trust swirling in her gaze. The tears in her eyes shone with reflected light.

At the same time, Takatsuki's eyes were also sparkling as he stared at Ayane... Though, of course, that was due to his curiosity.

Suddenly, Takatsuki leaned forward over the table and began to speak in an excited tone.

"Modern ghost stories are my area of expertise! As a normal story, the needles just falling is a little simple, but it makes for a wonderful ghost story!"

Ah, this could be bad, thought Naoya.

If an object of interest was placed in front of Takatsuki, he would throw himself at it without reservation. Ignoring other people's feelings and the circumstances surrounding the situation, he would become absorbed in it like a child.

Takatsuki himself seemed to believe that he did this because he "lacked common sense," but Naoya's theory was that the man's thoughts about his research may well be running out of control. In any case, it put other people off, and Takatsuki couldn't control it well on his own, so it was a burden on him. Somebody had to put a stop to it at a suitable time.

"I'm curious as to where these needles are coming from. Do you know how many needles there have been so far? If it matches the number of needles that were stabbed into the straw doll, that will tie up the story nicely, but— *Ouch!*"

Suddenly, Takatsuki let out a cry of pain. The table shook with a clatter. It seemed like Sasakura had kicked Takatsuki in the shin.

The professor glared at his friend tearfully.

"That hurt! What are you doing, Kenji?!"

"Shut up. You're being loud."

Sasakura himself spoke in a low voice.

"Calm down a little. You're the only one getting excited here."

"...Oh."

Looking back at Ayane, Takatsuki's expression turned into shame. Ayane was sitting with her back pressed into the back of her chair, as if she had been pushed away by Takatsuki's energy. She looked bewildered. So did Kotoko.

"I... I'm sorry, KenKen. I did it again, didn't I?"

"If you're going to apologize, say it to her, not me."

Sasakura jutted his chin toward Ayane.

"Um, well, I'm sorry, Miss Harasawa! Your story is very interesting, so I got all excited all of a sudden... But this is a difficult situation for you, so I apologize."

"Oh, no, it's okay... I'm just happy you believe me, Professor."

Ayane waved away the apology, but her face still looked a little off.

Apparently, just like Naoya, Sasakura was one of Takatsuki's sensible people. Since they had known each other for such a long time, Sasakura didn't show him any mercy.

After clearing his throat with a small *ahem*, as if to start the conversation over, Takatsuki said, "Um... Anyway, I believe your story, Miss Harasawa. I would really like to solve this mystery, but...there are some peculiarities."

Ayane frowned in response.

"What peculiarities?"

"It's strange that things are only happening to you and not to Miss Makimura. And even stranger—why needles?"

"Huh?"

Ayane blinked. Kotoko's expression showed that she, too, wasn't sure what the meaning of the question was.

Naoya and the others as well looked at Takatsuki in confusion.

Takatsuki explained.

"I felt a bit uneasy when I saw that the straw doll was stabbed not just with nails but also with needles. Because, as a rule, nails are used on straw dolls, you see. And even if we try to separate the matter of the doll from what's happening to Miss Harasawa, the question remains—why needles? In this day and age, needles aren't that common. In the past, hand sewing and mending was much more common, so needles and sewing kits were both quite familiar items. But now we really only use them to attach buttons, right? The average person doesn't have many opportunities to get their hands on a needle."

"Ah— But we—"

Ayane started to speak before snapping her mouth shut.

Takatsuki inclined his head, prompting her to continue, and Ayane and Kotoko shared a look.

It was Kotoko who opened her mouth to answer.

"Um... We were in the crafting club all the way through high school.

Aya and I both. So needles might be more familiar to us, comparatively speaking."

"But I don't remember handling any needles irresponsibly or anything! I've even been to the Festival of Broken Needles! So the only thing I can think of that caused this is..."

The straw doll.

"It really was a bad idea to use that picture as my phone background, wasn't it? It's like all the needles from the doll are coming back to me..."

Ayane's gaze roved anxiously, and her voice trembled. Kotoko pat her back to try to comfort her.

Crossing her arms over her chest, Ruiko hummed contemplatively.

"I wonder about that. Ordinarily, I'd say this is someone harassing you, but if that were the case... What would be the point in planting needles on someone? As some kind of warning?"

"...That doesn't make sense. A warning is meaningless if the target doesn't know what they're being warned against. From what I've heard, these guys are scared because they don't know why this is happening," Sasakura said.

Naoya turned to Takatsuki.

"Are there any other stories like Harasawa's? Ones about being cursed after seeing a straw doll—or being haunted by needles?"

"Good question. I know of some needle-related stories from the Edo period, but they don't quite fit this case. As for being cursed after seeing a straw doll... Well, it's not as if they saw the Hour of the Ox Ritual itself. We could have a huge problem if they did, though."

"What?"

"If you witness someone performing the Hour of the Ox Ritual, something bad will happen. There are various theories as to what that means, such as the effect of the curse disappearing or the curse hitting you instead. People also say that to avoid those bad outcomes, the person casting the curse has to kill the person who saw them."

Ayane and Kotoko both went white as a sheet at Takatsuki's commentary. The two girls took each other's hands and leaned in close to one another. Their faces weren't alike at all, but they looked like twin sisters. It seemed their being very close friends was the truth.

Ruiko turned to the girls with a calming smile.

"It's okay; what you saw wasn't an actual Hour of the Ox Ritual, right? There aren't many stories of people being cursed just from looking at a straw doll, so it's all good! Now, how about some cake? Here! It looks delicious, doesn't it?"

All three of the girls had ordered pastries with their drinks. Ruiko got a fruit tart, Ayane got chocolate cake, and Kotoko ordered a no-bake cheesecake. Because of the subject of their conversation, no one had touched their food yet.

At Ruiko's urging, the other two girls picked up their forks. Ruiko began eating her cake as well. Takatsuki looked over at Naoya.

"Fukamachi, you could have ordered some cake, too, you know? I'm paying."

"I told you: I'm not a fan of sweets."

Naoya pulled his own iced coffee toward himself as he replied.

"Speak for yourself, Professor. You have such a sweet tooth, you should have ordered cake or a parfait or something."

"This is hardly the appropriate time for that sort of thing."

"You care about appropriate timing? I didn't realize."

"...KenKen, I get the feeling Fukamachi is bullying me. Am I imagining things?"

"You're imagining things."

Takatsuki swirled his straw around in his iced tea in response to Naoya's and Sasakura's coldness. He seemed to be sulking.

Then—

"...Ow...!"

Suddenly, Ayane cried out in a small voice before covering her mouth with her hand.

Kotoko touched Ayane's shoulder, her expression surprised.

"Aya? What's wrong?"

"..."

Ayane didn't answer, but she did take her hand away from her mouth. Something red was dripping from the corner of her lips.

"Wha—?!"

Sasakura leaned over the table.

Ayane lowered her head and spat out the contents of her mouth onto the edge of her plate. Globs of what had just been chocolate cake came out along with bloody saliva. In the dark-brown mess, something shone momentarily—a flash of silver.

Takatsuki reached for it without hesitation, picking it up in his fingers.

"...A needle."

There in his grasp was a single sewing needle, broken in two.

"That was in the cake?! Hey, show me your mouth!"

Standing up, Sasakura held Ayane's chin in his hand and tilted her head back. He peered into her mouth.

"...All right, there's no other foreign object. Drink a little water, then show me your mouth again so I can check the wound."

Ayane followed his directions, letting Sasakura examine her again after sipping from her cup.

Kotoko, face pale, trembled and shook as she looked at her friend.

"Why...? Why is this happening...? I hate this; I'm so scared...!"

Kotoko began to cry, and Ruiko went to her side to comfort her.

In the meantime, the people around them had begun to chatter. A café employee approached their table nervously.

"Excuse me...? Um, is something the matter...?"

"Yeah, actually—"

Sasakura began to answer the employee's question, but Ayane gripped his arm with a quivering hand.

She ignored Sasakura when he looked down at her in surprise, instead bowing her head to the employee.

"No! It's not the café's fault; it's mine! All of it—it's my fault...!"

Her voice was shrill, the corners of her mouth still stained with blood.

Plink, plink.

Naoya, hearing a faint tinkling sound, looked down at the floor and nearly jumped out of his seat.

Dozens of red pins were strewn about Ayane's feet.

Ayane's injury didn't appear to be serious, but to be safe, Takatsuki decided to escort her to a clinic. She told them that the needle must have been inside the cake, and when she bit into it without noticing, the needle snapped and cut her mouth. It was good that she had spit it out, because things could have been much worse if she had swallowed it.

When the café employee heard that there was a needle inside the cake, he turned pale and called for the manager, but Ayane insisted the café was not at fault. She didn't want it to turn into a big incident, so for the time being, no reports were filed.

Takatsuki called for a taxi, helped Ayane and Kotoko into the back seat, and closed the car door behind them. Before getting into the passenger seat, he turned to look at Naoya.

"I'm sorry, Fukamachi. I invited you for a normal outing, and it turned into this. Maybe my daily wishes are too strong, and I've finally started summoning ghosts toward myself."

"...No, well, I don't mind. And shouldn't you be happy if that's the case, Professor?"

"Personally, I'm quite pleased, but I hate to see a student get hurt. But more importantly, Fukamachi—"

Taking a step toward Naoya, Takatsuki lowered his voice.

"What did you see with your powers of observation? Were they lying? Telling the truth?"

"They weren't lying... I don't think."

"That's a bit of a vague answer. Are you not sure?"

"No... At least, there were no lies in their words."

That much was certain. Neither of their voices had warped.

Hearing this, Takatsuki looked at the two girls in the taxi with a murmured *hmm*.

Leaning against Kotoko's shoulder, Ayane seemed close to tears. Kotoko was crying again, holding Ayane close.

"I see... Well, then she may really be haunted by needles. How troublesome."

As he stared at the two frightened girls, Takatsuki's eyes were once more tinged with blue.

That night, Naoya received a call from Takatsuki.

"Fukamachi, I have some work for you; is that all right?"

"What is it?"

"Well, it's about today's incident."

According to Takatsuki, Ayane's wound was minor, but both she and Kotoko were in quite a bit of shock. After being examined by a doctor, the two girls took a taxi home.

"Do you want me to look for that straw doll?"

"Ah, Ruiko and I will do that, so you don't have to. It's in the scope of her research, so. There's something else I need from you."

"What is it?"

"I want you to make some inquiries."

"Inquiries...?"

"I want to know, in detail, what those two are normally like. On campus, outside of campus, too."

Takatsuki elaborated.

"I had the feeling I'd seen them around campus before, so I dug up some memories. I realized I'd seen them many times from afar, and every time, they were always together. They seemed very close. Even when walking in a group of other girls, they appeared to cling to each other, like they might start holding hands at any moment."

Takatsuki could remember anything he saw with his own eyes in vivid detail. Even when he witnessed the chaotic sights on campus, he remembered it all perfectly. And apparently, his memories could just be leafed through later, like photos in an album.

"But lately, there's been a male student tagging along with the two of them, like an add-on. I haven't taught him before, so I don't know who he is. He was carrying a book that said INTRODUCTION TO ECONOMICS on it, so I'm thinking he's in the Economics Department. I remember seeing his face last year, so he's probably a second-year. I want to know who he is. Fukamachi, you're in the same year as the girls, so I wonder if you could find something out through friends?"

"I can't. I don't have any friends."

"Huh?"

Naoya could sense Takatsuki was tilting his head in confusion on the other end of the phone at the flat dismissal.

He thought perhaps it was something that someone like Takatsuki wouldn't be able to understand.

"No, well, I have some acquaintances—people I can talk with if we're in the same place. But no one I'm really *friends* with. I didn't even have plans to meet up with anyone this summer."

"..."

Takatsuki was suddenly quiet.

His silence was a problem for Naoya, since they were talking over the phone. He couldn't tell what kind of face the other man was making. Was he angry? Shocked? Sympathetic?

"Um, Professor?"

Timidly, Naoya spoke up, unable to bear the quiet.

"...I see. I understand."

Takatsuki finally replied, and more importantly, he said he understood.

Naoya sighed with relief. He had avoided having to talk to people. It was a pity he wouldn't be able to get paid, but not everyone was cut out for some kinds of work.

Though, he shouldn't have been so quick to relax.

"If that's the case, Fukamachi, then let's host a barbecue party together!"

"...Excuse me?"

This was Takatsuki he was dealing with, after all. A normal person like Naoya might never be able to understand how someone like Takatsuki thought. *Oh well.*

So in less than two weeks, the preparations for Takatsuki's "barbecue party" were complete.

According to Takatsuki, if it was difficult for Naoya to interrogate people individually, all they had to do was provide a place where he *could* do it. They would put on the barbecue as a social gathering for students in Folklore Studies II, and Naoya could make his inquiries there.

Most of the students in Folklore Studies II were Literature Department first-years. There had to be some people in the class who were friends with Ayane and Kotoko. Naoya might be able to glean some information about the pair from his classmates.

They put out the invitation through the college's social media. Seiwa University regularly used social media to share communications from courses. It was a convenient way to reach a lot of students at once.

Although, it was summer break. Many students went on long trips or visited their families. Nonetheless, more than thirty people responded to the sudden invitation showing interest in the event. Probably because Takatsuki was so popular with students.

So one day in early September at the barbecue rental spot in Shinkiba Park, Takatsuki's "exciting barbecue party" was held. Apparently, these days, barbecue rentals offered packages that included equipment and ingredients, so one could show up empty-handed and still join in. It was amazing.

"Wow, Professor, you really did put on this crazy event just because you wanted to gather information, huh...?"

"Isn't it better to enjoy ourselves when we can? And it's the summertime! What's a summer without a barbecue?"

Takatsuki smiled as he looked around at the students who were starting to prepare their grills. Even though it was a barbecue, the professor was still wearing a suit. Naoya wondered if he realized his clothes would probably smell like smoke and food later.

"I'm glad more students came than expected. Fukamachi, make sure you use this time to build relationships with everyone, too. It's an important memory for your first summer at university."

"...I mean, I don't really care about that kind of thing."

In truth, he would rather stay away from crowded places as much as possible.

Still, he was participating in the gathering for two reasons. First, because he was drawn by the chance to eat meat without paying a lot for it, since Takatsuki was shouldering the cost of the event. And second, because he was curious about Ayane and Kotoko. It was hard not to be curious about someone when they spit up a needle right in front of you.

The two girls were among the students who were setting up. As could be expected, neither of them seemed to be in high spirits.

"So they came, after all," Naoya said.

Takatsuki looked at the girls with an expression of agreement and nodded.

"Yep. Just as I thought."

"Huh?"

Naoya's head cocked to the side in confusion.

But Takatsuki just looked at Naoya and smiled without answering.

"Now, then. Let's try casually questioning everyone, shall we?"

"What...? We're really doing it?"

"Of course we are; that's why we're having this barbecue party! I'll go ask around over there, Fukamachi, so you go interrogate another group, okay? Just keep it casual, and don't let Miss Harasawa and Miss Makimura catch on to what you're doing! —Heeey, can I join you at that table?"

"Huh, Professor, hey, wai—"

Before Naoya could stop him, Takatsuki smiled like Naoya's childhood golden retriever and ran off to join a suitable group.

"Oh, Professor Takatsuki! Come on over!"

"Professor, what would you like to drink? I'll get it for you!"

"What do you want to eat, Professor? I'll grill whatever it is!"

Excited voices erupted from the table Takatsuki had joined. He had been surprisingly shrewd in his choice—his group was entirely made up of girls.

Reluctantly, Naoya looked around the venue for a table that still had open seats. As he did, his eyes lit upon a familiar head of brown hair. One of his language course classmates, a boy named Nanba Youichi. The person he had spoken to on the first day of Takatsuki's class.

"Hey, Fukamachi. Over here, over here, we have an open seat!"

Nanba beckoned to him, his tone seeming friendly. Looking closer, Naoya realized everyone at the table was in his language class.

"Yo, how have you been, Fukamachi? What did you do over break?"

"Well, it was hot, so I didn't do much... You went to the beach with everyone recently, right? How was it?"

"Ah, yeah, that. There were tons of jellyfish, so it was a bit hard to swim. And the ramen at the beach house was made by amateurs, so it was mushy, y'know? But eating it in a place like that somehow made it taste nice."

A smile spread over Nanba's face, which was noticeably tanner than it had been before the summer.

Usually, Nanba was someone Naoya would talk to if he ran into him, and they had eaten lunch together a few times. He was honest and sociable and didn't lie much, so he was easy for Naoya to interact with.

There were other students at their grill who hadn't gone to the beach, either. Many of them hadn't seen each other in weeks, and everybody was enjoying themselves.

"Even though we're not in a seminar, our class gets to have a barbecue party."

"Yeah, I'm so happy. I mean, Professor Takatsuki invited us!"

"If given the choice, I would have liked it to start in the evening instead of the day, though! Then we could be drinking, too, y'know? Right, Fukamachi?"

"...I think that probably wouldn't have been an option, since we're pretty much all still underage."

Even though they had only organized the event to do some digging, the students all seemed to be in high spirits. They were talking loudly and spiritedly, and so far, there had been no sign of any warping, so Naoya relaxed a little and quietly joined the conversations. As each table began grilling meat, a pleasant smell wafted into the air. Here and there across the stations, fierce competitions started to unfold among people with disposable chopsticks and plates in hand. Some people kept only eating pieces of meat, and raised voices sounded from various tables, telling them to "eat some vegetables!"

"I'm a growing boy! I want more meat; give it here!"

"What are you gonna do if you grow any taller?! I'm shorter; give the meat to me!"

"Hey, boys, eat your vegetables! You're all idiots, so you need to eat some green onions!"

Everyone sure is lively, Naoya thought, transferring some meat and vegetables from the serving tray onto the grill. Having lost big-time in a game of rock-paper-scissors, he was put in charge of grilling.

Surprisingly, he found himself enjoying it.

Everyone gathered at his table watched over the grill with bated breath as the food sizzled. When he noticed the ingredients starting to change color, Naoya flipped them over one by one starting from the beginning of the row. The other students still kept watch.

Then, when the meat was cooked just right, everyone's chopsticks shot forward at once with the speed of a chameleon's tongue snagging its food. Those who missed out on the meat reached for the vegetables in resignation, and they seemed to prefer the corn over the carrots and bell peppers.

Having grasped the situation after the first go, Naoya deliberately switched up where he placed the meat and vegetables to try to give people who failed to grab the meat last time a better chance. He made sure to figure out the timing so there wouldn't be much of a pause between rounds. This kind of position may be called a grill master, but it felt more like being a mama bird feeding hungry chicks.

"Hey, Nanba. That meat isn't ready yet. Put it back."

"Whaaat? It's fine! I like it like this!"

"Nope. You get a penalty for making a false start. Eat that pepper."

"Damn, you're strict, Fukamachi."

Then, looking up, Naoya saw Ayane and Kotoko at a table across the way, and he froze.

Crap. He had gotten so caught up in grilling that he almost forgot the reason they were here in the first place.

Just then, one of the girls offered to take over for him, and Naoya gratefully let her. He looked around timidly at the other students at his table.

"Um… By the way, is anyone here friends with Harasawa or Makimura?"

"Huh? Where'd that come from?"

Nanba cocked his head in confusion at Naoya's question.

"Um, well, it's just, when I went out the other day, I saw them crying. So I was just wondering if something had happened."

It wasn't like he could say he saw Ayane spit out a needle, after all, so he tried to explain without letting that unpleasant information slip.

Nanba looked even more puzzled.

"Fukamachi, are you friends with Harasawa and that group?"

"W-we aren't close, or anything… You could say we're acquaintances. We've just talked a little."

"If you mean Ayane Harasawa and Kotoko Makimura, I'm in the same club as them."

The girl who had taken over grilling for Naoya spoke up. He was pretty sure her surname was Aoki.

"Which club? Crafting?"

"No, English club. They're both nice girls; they hardly ever skip club activities."

Aoki skillfully placed meat on the grill as she spoke.

"Ah, but now that I think of it, they did say they were in the crafting club up through high school. You sure know a lot, Fukamachi."

"Oh yeah… I heard them talking once about doing crafts as a hobby."

"But it seems like they still carry around sewing kits, I guess? Ayane dropped some pins once. Right when she got up from her chair, pins came tumbling down. When I asked her what happened, she said the hem of her skirt was frayed, and she had pinned it up temporarily and forgotten about it. It kinda surprised me, though, like, who would do that sort of thing, usually? If you were in the crafting club, you could sew it up in no time, right?"

"Ah...I see..."

By chance, Naoya had encountered eyewitness testimony regarding Ayane being haunted by needles. Saying she had used pins to temporarily fix her hem didn't really seem like an effective way to not appear suspicious to the people around her.

"Hey, Aoki. Do you happen to know who those two are friends with?"

"Hmm... Everyone in our club gets along pretty well, I think. Although, Ayane and Kotoko are always attached at the hip, so I don't know if there's anyone else... The only person who comes to mind is Takasu. He's a second-year. That's a bit different, though, I guess."

"Different, how?"

"Takasu is an upperclassman in our club. He and Ayane started dating around May. He's a nice person, so he's careful about not hurting Ayane and Kotoko's relationship. Apparently, he even invited Kotoko to join him and Ayane on a date."

"Ah... I see. So does that mean Makimura isn't dating anyone?"

"Kotoko? No, I don't think she is. She's a lot shyer than Ayane."

"Right..."

Just in case, Naoya also asked what department Takasu was in. He really wanted to ask for Takasu's contact info, but it would have been weird to go that far.

Suddenly, Naoya was thumped hard in the side, making him jump.

"Wh-what are you doing, Nanba?"

"Fukamachi. Could it be? Are you blossoming?"

"What?"

Fixing his dislodged glasses, Naoya looked back at Nanba.

The other boy chuckled creepily and grabbed Naoya by the shoulders.

"Which one? Which girl are you into? Harasawa? No, she's spoken for. Is it Makimura?"

"...Nanba, it's not like that, okay?"

Naoya removed Nanba's hands as he answered.

But Nanba was undeterred and grabbed at him again.

"Aw, come on! You hardly ever ask about other people! Or it's not like you to do that, more like. You don't seem interested in anyone else, usually."

"Oh..."

Nanba's words were surprisingly dead-on, and Naoya was momentarily shocked into silence.

"W-well, that's because, um—"

He tried to think of some excuse, but Nanba shook his head.

"I'm relieved to see you're just as curious about the people around you as anyone else would be. I mean, I was surprised to see you here today. You should come to more of our drinking parties and stuff, you know? I know you never come because of money, but I found a cheap place we can go, so—"

"Ah... Yeah. S-sorry..."

As they talked, more meat had been cooked and was ready to eat.

In an instant, the expression in Nanba's eyes changed. He drew his chopsticks with the quickness of a bolt of lightning. But the other students didn't intend to lose, either. Having already fought this battle countless times, they had learned each other's tendencies and movements. Multiple chopsticks met over the grill top, and after a fierce fight, a piece of meat flicked off someone's chopsticks and into the air. People started yelling, and without thinking, Naoya screamed along with them, chasing the still airborne meat with his chopsticks.

Takatsuki had told him to build some relationships, and Naoya had said he didn't care to. He didn't need summer memories or friends.

But...he couldn't deny that this wasn't so bad, really.

*   *   *

As the barbecue party was wrapping up, Takatsuki and Naoya met in front of the restroom to report their findings.

"I'll go first."

Takatsuki raised his hand slightly.

"Several of the students said they had seen Miss Harasawa's phone background when it was the picture of the straw doll. They said she changed the picture reluctantly because people were telling her it was in poor taste. It seems Miss Harasawa is a rather spirited girl who likes to do strange things, and Miss Makimura watches over her antics from the sidelines while admonishing her with a smile. They both went to the same private all-girls high school, and apparently Miss Makimura wanted to go straight on to the affiliated women's college. But because Miss Harasawa wanted to come here, Miss Makimura changed her plans and came to Seiwa as well. Miss Makimura is seemingly always saying 'I'm helpless without Aya,' but according to the girls around them, it's Miss Harasawa who is helpless without Miss Makimura."

As expected, Takatsuki had been able to question the girls' group he had joined because he was so popular with them. He had gathered a lot of information.

"They're awfully close, they're in the same club, and they usually do everything together. The other girls said it's like they continued on with the vibe from their all-girls school, but I wonder if that's what all-girls schools are like? Incidentally, it seems the reason they're in my class isn't because they have an interest in folklore, but because of my looks."

He had gathered some trivial information while he was at it. Though, Naoya suspected that most of the girls in his class were taking it for the same reason.

"But as for the male student who recently started hanging out with Miss Harasawa and Miss Makimura, none of the girls in my group knew anything about him. Only that they had seen him before. Is no one interested in who their friends are dating?"

"Ah, I figured that out in my group. He's Harasawa's boyfriend. He's a second-year in the same club named Takasu."

It was Naoya's turn to raise his hand and add on to Takatsuki's information.

"Ah, so someone in your group did know something. So Miss Harasawa is the one he's going out with?"

"Yes. But apparently he's wary of getting in the way of their friendship, so he invites Makimura to come along with them on dates."

"I wonder if that way of handling things is the right choice... And? Did you learn anything else?"

"A girl in the same club as Harasawa and Makimura saw pins fall from Harasawa's skirt. Harasawa told her she had used pins to temporarily fix a frayed hem."

"That's a bit far-fetched as an explanation, isn't it? But then, just as you said, the two of them weren't lying. Miss Harasawa really is being haunted by needles," Takatsuki said.

"Is it the curse of the straw doll, after all?" Naoya asked.

"Yeah... In a way, I suppose you could say that."

Takatsuki's reply was vague. Naoya wondered if the professor had already figured out what was going on.

"Professor, what are you planning to do? An exorcism or something?"

"I wonder. It seems we're already at a point where we can't just let things be. If we don't do something—"

But something interrupted him.

"—Huh, oh no, hey, are you okay?!"

Someone was shouting.

Looking over at the barbecue area, they could see a girl crouching down, clutching her arm. The other students were gathered around her anxiously.

Takatsuki murmured.

"That's...Miss Makimura."

"What, Makimura?!"

Takatsuki immediately broke into a run toward her. Naoya followed.

When they reached the table, it was indeed Kotoko they saw stooped low to the ground. Her left sleeve was rolled up to her shoulder. One glance at her was enough to see what was wrong—her left bicep was bright red and inflamed.

"What happened? Did you get burned?"

Takatsuki questioned her, but the one who answered was Ayane, who stood at Kotoko's side, her face pale.

"No. Kotoko suddenly grabbed her arm and looked like she was in pain... When I rolled up her sleeve, her arm was all red and swollen...!"

"Let me take a look."

Takatsuki knelt beside Kotoko and took her arm. He leaned in close, examining the swollen area carefully—then, suddenly, he frowned.

"P-Professor? What is it?"

Ayane's voice shook.

Looking up at Ayane, Takatsuki gave her a smile.

"Somehow or other, it seems Miss Makimura was **stung by a bee.**"

Takatsuki's voice warped. Startled, Naoya put his hands over his ears without thinking.

Takatsuki had just told a lie.

She hadn't been stung by a bee. Or at least, Takatsuki didn't think she had.

But a slight sense of relief fell over the group of very anxious students surrounding them. Seeing that, Naoya remembered what Takatsuki had told him before, about people fearing the unexplained. A mysterious swelling was creepy and scary, but if it was chalked up to a simple bee-sting, the group was more likely to calm down and think, "A bee, huh?"

Standing back up, Takatsuki looked around at the students.

"They should have a first-aid kit in the management office over there, so I'll take Miss Makimura over. The rest of you should start to clean up here."

At Takatsuki's words, the group erupted into chatter—"What, seriously?" "Were there bees around here?"—and returned to their separate tables.

Takatsuki used his hands to support Kotoko's shoulders and help her stand, then he looked at Ayane.

"Miss Harasawa, do you have a sewing kit on you?"

"Huh? I do, but..."

"Does it have tweezers in it?"

"A small pair, but yes."

"Good. Then grab it and come with me. You too, Fukamachi."

They walked like that with Takatsuki supporting Kotoko—and Ayane and Naoya following behind.

Takatsuki found a bench out of sight of the barbecue area and had Kotoko sit there.

Ayane looked puzzled.

"Huh, Professor, weren't we going to go to the management office?"

"Yes, we're going. We'll need to get this sterilized. But before that, I need to check something. Miss Harasawa, your tweezers, please."

Once again, Takatsuki reached for Kotoko's arm. With his fingers, he pressed carefully against the inflamed skin.

Kotoko screwed up her face, and something small could be seen pushing out of her skin.

Using the tweezers, Takatsuki nimbly pulled out the object.

It was a needle.

A small silver sewing needle.

As soon as she saw it, Kotoko let out a small moan. Her pale face crumpled, and her eyes filled with tears as the others looked on.

At Naoya's side, Ayane sank down hard in shock. Covering her mouth with trembling hands, she began to speak in a shrill voice.

"Why...? Why Kotoko, too...?!"

Kotoko looked at Ayane from her seat on the bench.

"Aya..."

On the verge of breaking down into tears, Kotoko reached out a hand toward her friend.

Blood swelled up into a bead at the spot on her arm where Takatsuki had removed the needle. Before long, the bead of blood turned into a single trickling drop that flowed down her pale arm, reaching all the way to the hand she held outstretched toward Ayane.

"Hey, Aya, what should I do...?"

Ayane stared, trembling, at the blood dripping from Kotoko's fingertips. Then, all at once, as if coming to her senses, she reached out and grabbed on to her friend's hand.

"Kotoko! Kotoko, it's okay, it's going to be all right... It's okay...!"

Knees shaking, Ayane stood, then sat down beside Kotoko on the bench. Like that, she wrapped her arms around the other girl and started to cry.

Naoya watched them, feeling utterly baffled.

The curse was spreading. And not just spreading. It was getting worse.

It had started out with needles just falling around, and now people were getting hurt.

What was Takatsuki thinking? Naoya wondered. How would he interpret this mystery?

Naoya looked at the professor.

Takatsuki was staring at the needle he had just extracted with great interest. He looked exactly like an entomologist who had obtained a precious specimen.

Why does it look like he's smiling? Naoya thought with a shiver.

"P-Professor?"

Without meaning to, he spoke up.

Takatsuki looked at him.

When he did, he was well and truly smiling.

"Hey, Fukamachi. I know a story terribly similar to this one."

"What...?"

Naoya's eyes widened with surprise.

Takatsuki carefully wrapped the sewing needle in a handkerchief and tucked it into his pocket before turning to kneel in front of the girls on the bench. He peered into their faces from up close, then spoke in a gentle voice.

"Miss Harasawa. Miss Makimura. Somehow, the situation has

become quite serious. We can't let things go on like this. So let's do an exorcism."

"E-exorcism?"

"Would you be the one doing it, Professor...?"

Ayane and Kotoko were blinking at him in surprise.

Takatsuki smiled and nodded.

"I'd like the two of you to come to my office tomorrow. Fukamachi, you come, too, okay?"

When Naoya arrived at Takatsuki's office the next day, Ayane and Kotoko were already there. Takatsuki was nowhere to be found.

The girls, their faces tense, were sitting on folding chairs at the center table. White gauze was taped to Kotoko's left arm.

"...Come to think of it, why are *you* here?"

Brow furrowing slightly, Ayane scowled at Naoya. Kotoko tugged at the edge of Ayane's clothes, scolding her with an "Aya." But Kotoko was also looking at Naoya with a little suspicion in her eyes. Well, as far as the two of them were concerned, Naoya was just an unrelated party who happened to be there when they asked Takatsuki for help.

The night before, Naoya had received a call from Takatsuki.

He wanted to talk about why Naoya would be present at the exorcism.

Takatsuki had asked Naoya to tell him if the girls lied.

"If you notice the two of them lying while I do the exorcism, I want you to give me a signal. Something as natural as possible; something they won't notice. How about, if Miss Harasawa tells a lie, touch your right ear, and if Miss Makimura lies, touch your left ear?"

But it wasn't like Naoya could tell the girls that. He sat in a chair apart from them, in silence, feeling a bit uncomfortable.

"Ah, sorry I'm late! Thank goodness, everyone is already here!"

Right then, Takatsuki opened the office door and walked into the room.

He looked over the three of them seated at the center table and smiled.

"Well then, shall we begin? Can each of you take one of these, please?"

As he said that, he handed the several sheets of paper he had been holding to Ayane, who was closest.

Ayane frowned, looking doubtful.

"Huh? What is this...? Are we not doing the exorcism?"

"No, we are! That's why I had you come here, after all."

Takatsuki was still smiling brightly.

Looking at the paper Kotoko had passed him, Naoya also felt confused. It was just like the materials Takatsuki used in his lectures. It was an old story that seemed to have been copied from some book.

"Right, starting now, I will be exorcizing Miss Harasawa and Miss Makimura."

After making that declaration, Takatsuki sat down in the chair across from Ayane and Kotoko.

The girls looked at each other, baffled. There was nothing in the office that fit the image of an exorcism. Takatsuki was wearing a suit as usual, and the office was filled with the scent of old books. It was still summer vacation, so it was quiet on campus.

In the silence, Takatsuki's voice echoed softly.

"Even though I say 'exorcism,' I'm not an exorcist, so I'm going to do this in the style of a lecture. This strange incident involving needles that's happening to Miss Harasawa and Miss Makimura—there's a similar story that appears in a book from the Edo period. That's what's on the materials I just handed you. The book is called *Mikikigusa*, and it was written by a man named Seishin Miyazaki. It contains accounts of incidents and disasters from that time period, as well as romantic and scary stories that Miyazaki collected. Among them is a story he recorded under the title 'Mysterious Illness.'"

The two girls, still looking perplexed, glanced down at the papers in their hands. However, the story copied to the papers seemed to have come straight from a book that was published during the Edo period, and because it hadn't been printed, it was difficult to read.

Takatsuki continued talking.

"Well, I'll have you read the materials thoroughly later, but I'll give you a brief introduction as to what the story is about… A fourteen-year-old girl named Ume complained of pains all over her body. Then, when someone poked at a spot where it hurt, the tip of a needle popped out from under her skin."

Kotoko's shoulders jolted. The exact same thing had happened to her only a day before.

"Several needles were recovered from various parts of Ume's body. The nape of her neck, her knees, vulva, solar plexus, and mixed in with the saliva from her mouth, as well. The symptoms began when Ume began apprenticing under a pharmacist named Matsuya. They attempted to treat her without success, and ultimately, she was sent home from her apprenticeship. She recovered after convalescing for a while at home, so the following year, she began a new apprenticeship, but her condition worsened soon after. When her mother was asked if she had any idea what might be causing the illness, she said that around the time Ume left to be Matsuya's apprentice, a group of weasels ran all around Ume while she slept and urinated in great quantities beneath her futon, and maybe that was the source. She also said it could have been the work of another trickster spirit, like a fox or a tanuki. Of course, from a modern perspective, the mother's answer is nonsense. Needles coming out of someone's body has nothing to do with the existence of foxes, tanuki, or weasel spirits. But at the time, that explanation was plausible. In those days, it was common for people to think strange illnesses were caused by being possessed by foxes. That was their interpretation of the situation."

Come to think of it, Takatsuki had told Naoya once that the unexplained was made up of two things: phenomenon and interpretation.

People in the past interpreted the phenomenon of needles coming out of the body as a strange consequence of foxes and tanuki making mischief. That was as good an explanation as any, for people without a sufficient knowledge of science or medicine.

"But…we're not possessed by foxes or tanuki or weasels."

Ayane spoke up.

"This is Tokyo. There aren't any animals like that here, Professor. What are we supposed to be getting from this story?"

She glared sharply at Takatsuki.

"Aya," Kotoko said, tugging on her friend's clothes again.

"Well, tanuki and weasels are found even in Tokyo, you know. But what you're saying is understandable, Miss Harasawa. We have to approach this mystery with a modern interpretation."

Not at all perturbed by Ayane's scowl, Takatsuki kept smiling.

"A mysterious condition where needles come out of the body. A condition that only surfaces when the sufferer is living as an apprentice—and that goes away when she returns home. A normal interpretation would postulate that this is a case of cruel mistreatment. Perhaps the fellow apprentices, or else the lord or lady of the house, stuck needles into the body of the new apprentice girl as a form of punishment. That would be a reasonable assessment... But I think there's another possibility."

"What is it?"

"I think it's possible that Ume stabbed the needles into her own body."

At Takatsuki's words, the two girls stiffened up.

Takatsuki was still smiling. Even though what he was saying was horribly gruesome, his radiant smile didn't budge.

"The reason being: Ume was sent home from her apprenticeship thanks to her mysterious condition. When she recovered and was once again sent off to work, the same condition resurfaced, and again she was sent home. It's quite reasonable to speculate that Ume stabbed herself with the needles because she wanted to go home. Maybe she couldn't adapt to her apprenticeship, or maybe she was being bullied. Perhaps she just wanted sympathy from those around her. Whatever the reason, I can't rule out the possibility that a desperate fourteen-year-old girl would take a needle from a sewing kit and either swallow it or stab herself with it."

There was a small crinkling sound.

Ayane was gripping the edge of the paper Takatsuki had handed out. The paper was crumpled in her grasp.

"…In other words, Professor, you're saying we did this to ourselves?"

"Yes. That's exactly right."

Takatsuki nodded.

Immediately, Ayane's cheeks flushed crimson. Beneath her tightly drawn brows, her strong-willed eyes were glaring furiously at Takatsuki.

"How cruel. Kotoko and I have both been injured. How could you say such a horrible thing, Professor?!"

"Naturally, I don't think all of it was self-inflicted. But at the very least, this isn't a straw doll curse."

As he spoke, Takatsuki placed a single photo on the table.

It was the picture Ayane had submitted with her report. It was dark and hard to make out, but it was just possible to see the dim image in the center of a straw doll with nails and needles stuck into it.

Takatsuki pointed at the straw doll.

"Because this photo…is a fake."

Ayane's eyes widened dramatically at his frank assertion. In an instant, the blood drained from her scarlet cheeks.

Takatsuki continued in a calm tone.

"You bought this doll yourself and stuck it with nails and needles, right? And the story that you saw it in Hibiya Park was also a lie, wasn't it?"

"It… **It wasn't a lie!**"

Ayane's screaming voice distorted violently.

Naoya grimaced and touched his right ear. If Ayane tells a lie, touch the right ear. That was the signal for Takatsuki.

Takatsuki glanced at Naoya before carrying on.

"If it's not a lie, can you tell me where in the park you saw it? You said you were heading home from a concert at the time. What concert did you see?"

"That's… **I don't remember anymore! It was ages ago! And the park is big; I don't remember exactly where!**"

Her voice was still extremely warped. Everything she was saying was a lie.

Naoya continued to touch his right ear, wondering what was going on. The straw doll story was a lie. He asked himself why he hadn't realized that before, but then he soon understood. When he first heard the story, it wasn't Ayane who had recounted it. It was Takatsuki. Naoya could only discern lies when they came directly from the source.

If Ayane had told the story herself, he would have known, but he couldn't tell if the contents of a story were untruthful just from someone else reading it aloud.

"Can I tell you my honest impression of this picture from when I first saw it? It was, 'Oh, this is a fake.' First of all, it's done incorrectly, using both nails and needles to pierce the doll. Today we have computers at hand to look up anything we want, so if you really wanted to curse someone, ordinarily you would look up the proper method. Also, a shrine somewhere would have been fine, but as a location, Hibiya Park is pretty careless. The real kicker is that this doesn't look like it's been nailed to a tree. You might have thought I wouldn't be able to tell because the background was darkened, but it looks like it was placed on the ground. Although it's not like I analyzed the image or anything, so I can't confirm that."

Takatsuki had been suspecting Ayane's story was fake ever since she had submitted the photo along with her report.

Thinking it over, if Takatsuki had believed the straw doll story, he probably would have called Ayane to his office just as he had Naoya. Also, looking back on when they had first heard the story in Yanaka, Takatsuki hadn't seemed all that keen on straw dolls. It made sense, if he thought it was all a hoax.

"This kind of thing is Miss Ruiko's specialty, so I had her read Miss Harasawa's report. She came to the same conclusion, that it was just a made-up story. Nevertheless, I had her do some research for me for the time being. She scoured the internet to see if there were any other stories of people seeing straw dolls at Hibiya Park—and even went with me to the site to investigate. But our conclusions didn't change.

There were no other eyewitness accounts aside from Miss Harasawa's, and there were no traces of anything at the site. Moreover—you said it yourself in Yanaka, didn't you? 'It's like all the needles from the doll are coming back to me...' 'Coming back' only makes sense to say if you're the person who stuck the needles in the doll."

Ayane didn't reply. Her face was bright red again, and she was glowering at Takatsuki.

It seemed Takatsuki was correct. Who knew if she wanted the extra credit, or to get Takatsuki's attention, or if it was just a simple prank? Regardless, she had really made herself a nuisance.

But suddenly, Naoya frowned.

Just a little while ago, Takatsuki had said "...I don't think all of it was self-inflicted."

Which meant...

"Now, let's get back to talking about needles instead of straw dolls, okay? From the beginning, it wasn't the doll that interested me, it was this."

Again as he spoke, Takatsuki placed something on the table.

It was a small plastic bag with two needles inside.

They seemed to be the broken needle that Ayane had spit out and the one that came from Kotoko's arm.

"After submitting her report on the straw doll, Miss Harasawa began to experience needles falling from all around her body. This matter isn't related to the straw doll, but you could say it was inspired by it. The common thread is, yes, needles."

Takatsuki picked up the plastic bag with his fingers. Inside the bag, the needles shifted as if to show off their sharp points.

"Miss Ruiko said it herself that day in the café. 'Ordinarily, I'd say this is someone harassing you...' Since the straw doll wasn't genuine, of course this mystery would be a hoax as well. And when it comes to people near Miss Harasawa who have a connection to needles, well... There's only one person who comes to mind, isn't there?"

Takatsuki smiled and pointedly tilted his head.

The person he had turned his gaze on—was Kotoko.

Ayane turned her piercing gaze on the other girl.

Kotoko said nothing. She just kept looking straight up at Takatsuki.

Takatsuki went on.

"Both of you were in the crafting club, right? And when Miss Harasawa cooked up the straw doll idea, you were with her, weren't you, Miss Makimura? Because you're always together. Maybe you even stabbed it with needles together. Miss Harasawa was just playing around, making a fake straw doll, taking its picture, making the picture her phone background, and at her side—Miss Makimura, what were you thinking?"

Takatsuki's eyes bored into Kotoko. Ayane's gaze was fixed on her as well.

Suddenly, Kotoko let out a small "Heh."

She looked like she was laughing.

"I mean… Aya doesn't listen to me even if I tell her she shouldn't do something."

Her tone didn't change at all. Her voice was gentle, mild-mannered, sweet.

But her facial expression had changed completely.

For a girl like Kotoko to have eyes that looked like that… Staring at her, Naoya felt fear. There was sweet poison in her gaze.

She started to speak.

"Straw dolls are for cursing people, right? I didn't think it was right to fool around with one. So I thought maybe it would be good for her to have a bit of a scare, just a little one. It's like you said, Professor. After Aya stood up, I would secretly scatter pins on her chair, then I would say something. Like, 'Aya, there are needles everywhere. What's going on?' It was only supposed to be a little prank. Ah-ha."

Kotoko laughed a little as if remembering.

Ayane's expression hardened. Narrowing her eyes at her friend, Kotoko continued talking.

"But, Aya, you looked so bewildered. Even though you had fun making a straw doll yourself, you can be surprisingly cowardly at times. So

I said, 'Oh no, maybe the needles you stabbed into the straw doll are coming back for you. You really shouldn't have done something like that as a game.'"

Kotoko's voice didn't warp in the slightest.

She really had said those things to Ayane. She truly did act like the needles she had planted herself were the consequence of the straw doll's curse.

"Ah—that is precisely what a curse is."

Takatsuki picked up the photograph of the straw doll again.

"Straw dolls are used to cast curses. It's wrong to use them as toys. That knowledge is deeply rooted in most Japanese people. That's why people feel like they've done something taboo after playing around with such things or just dabbling in them. Miss Makimura struck on that feeling within Miss Harasawa. Her words turned the fake straw doll into a real one. Miss Harasawa believed her, and the curse became a reality. She interpreted the phenomenon of needles appearing around her as the result of the straw doll's curse."

The unexplained was made up of two things: phenomenon and interpretation.

Unexplained phenomena are frightening. People are afraid of what they don't understand. That's why they interpret their realities.

Kotoko had guided Ayane toward a misleading interpretation. If, at the time, she had said, "Maybe someone is bullying you?" even Ayane wouldn't have thought she was cursed.

"But, Miss Makimura," Takatsuki said. "Why didn't you stop scattering needles around your friend? If you only wanted to scare her a little, surely doing it a few times would have been plenty."

Kotoko went back to being silent.

Takatsuki narrowed his eyes slightly. His gaze casually swept over to Naoya. Keeping his eyes on Naoya, Takatsuki continued to direct his words at Kotoko.

"Maybe you felt good seeing Miss Harasawa scared? I wonder if you would say the relationship between you is always equal. Is Miss

Harasawa, who can be a bit pushy, the slightly superior one? Or maybe it has something to do with Miss Harasawa getting a boyfriend?"

"You're wrong."

At that point, Kotoko's voice started to distort. Naoya touched his left ear.

He saw Takatsuki stop speaking for a moment and take a small breath.

Once more, the professor fixed his gaze on Kotoko.

"Miss Makimura. You and Miss Harasawa were always together. Always together—and very close. But when you entered university, Miss Harasawa got a boyfriend. Your relationship with her was deteriorating. You couldn't let that happen, right?"

"You're wrong."

Face stiff, Kotoko shook her head. As before, her denial twisted and warped.

"I expect needles are familiar and very memorable objects to the two of you. You were in the crafting club together for all that time. The straw doll was probably what got you thinking about leaving needles around Miss Harasawa. But within that, I suspect, was the message, 'Don't forget about me.'"

"You're wrong!"

Kotoko's third denial tore at Naoya's eardrums with a metallic screech. Naoya kept his hand pressed to his left ear as his face twisted.

As he did, he thought about the feelings of the girl who had strewn needles around her best friend.

He imagined what it felt like to Kotoko when she couldn't help but curse her closest friend, who she was supposed to love.

They were so close that she had changed her own future plans so they could go to the same college. So close that everyone around them thought: Ayane must have Kotoko, and Kotoko must have Ayane.

It was like their own little paradise. A world no one else could enter, a happy place with just the two of them. Kotoko might have thought that would continue forever.

But things changed when they left their all-girls high school and went to a coed university.

Ayane got a boyfriend.

Another living person—one of a different gender, no less—came into what should have been their private paradise.

Out loud, Kotoko had almost certainly said, "How nice." Maybe even, "I'm so glad you got such a cool boyfriend." Ayane's boyfriend was a kind upperclassman. He even looked out for Kotoko's feelings and invited her to join them on a date. What was Kotoko really feeling during that date?

Was she concealing needles in her hand, waiting to scatter them in a chair after Ayane stood up—or onto her skirt?

Small needles wouldn't hurt someone seriously. But with their sharp points, they certainly could make someone feel threatened.

Don't forget. You're mine forever.

Don't leave me behind. We're supposed to be together forever.

If Kotoko really had been thinking those things while she sowed her needles, then it was definitely a curse.

Her own special incantation to keep Ayane at her side.

"However, Miss Harasawa is no fool. It didn't take her long to realize that the needles were Miss Makimura's doing," Takatsuki said.

Kotoko's shoulders jolted, and she turned to look at her friend.

Ayane was wearing a somewhat exasperated expression.

"…It was so obvious; of course I would notice."

Her voice was low.

"I mean, the needles only appeared when I was with Kotoko. They never did when I was by myself."

"Aya… Then…at the café—the time in Yanaka…"

Kotoko's voice was trembling.

Ayane nodded.

"Yes. I put the needle in the cake at the café in Yanaka. I put it in my own cake."

Her confession came out in a rush.

Her voice didn't distort at all.

"Right. That was the day this story got complicated," Takatsuki declared.

That day, a chance encounter between Takatsuki and the girls changed the situation.

Having caught on to Kotoko's actions, instead of telling her directly to cut it out, Ayane had the idea to get Takatsuki involved.

"It caused trouble for the café, so I can't condone what you did, but, well... Your approach was rather original and interesting, Miss Harasawa. By consulting me, you could label the story of the needles as a mere mystery. You tried to make it the straw doll's curse, rather than Miss Makimura's work. In doing so, you were, for the time being, protecting her."

When Takatsuki said "protecting," Kotoko glanced at Ayane again.

Ayane didn't return her gaze, but she also didn't refute Takatsuki's claim.

"And then, to top it off, you ate the needle yourself. It's the kind of act that makes you wonder how someone could do it, but Miss Harasawa must have felt like she had no choice. You're the kind of person who speaks her mind. But even so, you couldn't tell Miss Makimura 'stop' to her face. Rather than accuse and reproach your friend, you chose to make yourself bleed. You probably thought it would shock Miss Makimura into stopping... And in fact, Miss Makimura did receive a shock. Why had a needle come out of Miss Harasawa's cake, when she hadn't put it there herself? It must have been quite a surprise."

Kotoko's fear and confusion when she saw Ayane spit out the needle had been real. She had looked as though she had seen a ghost.

"Of course, later, Miss Makimura also realized it had been Miss Harasawa's own doing. But at that point, the story became a very serious matter. Miss Harasawa had gotten me involved and spat out a needle in front of several other people, so it was no longer something that could end as nothing but a minor prank."

Ayane's actions had driven Kotoko into a corner.

By putting the needle in her own mouth, she had called out Kotoko. But Kotoko had probably thought she was the only one who realized the message behind that incident. Because at the time, the tide of events was flowing entirely toward the idea of the straw doll's curse.

"And so Miss Makimura decided to take advantage of the barbecue party I held. Just like Miss Harasawa, in front of other people, to show her friend that she herself had been cursed by needles—she inserted the needle into her own body, to settle everything as the fault of the curse."

After Takatsuki had extracted the needle, Kotoko had said, "...What should I do...?"

There hadn't been any distortion in her voice. She really hadn't known what to do anymore.

She stabbed her own body with the needle. What on earth had that felt like?

To want to do something about the circumstances in front of her, but not be able to think of any other way?

Ayane and Kotoko both took up needles and harmed themselves.

Ah, Naoya thought.

It was just as Takatsuki had said. Ume in *Mikikigusa*. If she had stuck the needles into her own body, perhaps she had felt the same way these two girls did.

Unable to express herself honestly to the people around her, she stabbed herself with small, thin, sharp needles, hoping it would change something.

Some who saw it would say she had a mysterious illness. Some would say she was cursed. Some kind of divine punishment.

But the truth—the *reality* might have been something like this.

"...Aya," Kotoko said.

Ayane stared at her. Kotoko's mouth snapped shut, as if intimidated by her friend's blank gaze. Withdrawing the shaking hand she had stretched toward Ayane, Kotoko hung her head. One at a time, large teardrops welled up in her eyes and fell.

Seeing that, for a moment, Ayane's face faltered.

Head still bowed, Kotoko spoke.

"I'm sorry, Aya... I'm sorry, I'm so sorry... I did something stupid. I'm really sorry..."

"You really are a dummy," Ayane whispered.

Kotoko's shoulders shook in surprise.

But Ayane reached for her trembling shoulders and held them.

"You should have just told me if you didn't like Takasu. You're so stupid, dummy... But it's okay now."

Ayane hugged Kotoko as she talked.

"You like me so much that you thought of all that."

"Aya..."

In Ayane's arms, Kotoko lifted her head and started to sob.

Ayane laughed, gently patting Kotoko's hair.

"It's all right. **I forgive you, Kotoko.**"

Ayane's voice warped violently as she peered into Kotoko's face.

Naoya shuddered and, without thinking, pressed his hands to his ears.

"...Fukamachi?"

Takatsuki was looking at Naoya. Unable to answer, Naoya stared at the two girls, dumbfounded.

They were hugging, their arms wrapped around one another's backs.

"No, Aya. **I'm the one who was wrong. You didn't do anything.**"

"**That's not true. I think I'm at fault here. I neglected you.**"

"Let's be friends forever, okay? **I'll never do anything to hurt you again.**"

"**Of course. We'll always, always be friends...**"

Their exchanged promises warped into a chaotic dissonance. *I don't blame you at all. It was my fault. We'll be friends forever.*

They lied, over and over and over.

Naoya felt dizzy.

Nothing they were saying was true. Nothing was actually resolved.

But the two of them held one another like they were acting out a passionate movie scene, spitting up nothing but sweet, gentle lines back and forth. In twisted voices that sounded like the warbling cacophony a broken record player would produce.

It was awful. Nauseating. The warping voices penetrated Naoya's eardrums. It felt like they were assaulting his brain, making it churn wildly. He couldn't stop shaking.

Stop it. Don't make me listen to your vulgar voices.

I don't want to see for myself just how foul human beings are, that they can lie as easily as they breathe.

Naoya covered his ears with both hands and looked down. He could hear Takatsuki calling his name, but his head was so heavy that he couldn't look up. He felt so terrible. Bit by bit, his consciousness was slipping away. He felt someone put a hand on his shoulder. Takatsuki's voice was in his ear. "Fukamachi, are you all right?" Those words—in that clear, beautiful voice—were all he could hear.

He tried to maintain consciousness by clinging to that voice, but it was no use. Naoya felt his body slump over as his consciousness tumbled down into the bottomless dark.

When he came to, Naoya found himself lying on a rudimentary couch made from several folding chairs pushed together.

When he tried to get up, he heard Takatsuki's voice.

"Don't get up yet. You should lie down a little longer."

Nevertheless, Naoya managed to sit up, causing a damp handkerchief to fall from his forehead. It probably belonged to Takatsuki. Naoya's glasses had been removed and placed on the table.

Takatsuki was sitting on the edge of the table, looking down at Naoya worriedly. Ayane and Kotoko were no longer in the office.

"You collapsed suddenly, and it surprised them. But for now, you and I have done all we can for them, so I sent them home."

As he spoke, Takatsuki held out a small plastic bottle that had been left beside him. It was mineral water.

"Drink it if you feel up to it. I think it'll make you feel a bit better."

The bottle was well chilled and covered in condensation. It looked like it had been bought from a vending machine. Naoya gratefully accepted it and took a drink.

"I'm sorry, Fukamachi."

Out of nowhere, Takatsuki apologized to him.

Naoya stared back at his professor. His vision wasn't that bad, even without his glasses. In truth, his glasses weren't even that strong. He only wore them because, for some reason, he wanted to view the world through glass.

Takatsuki looked at Naoya with his eyebrows lowered and a truly remorseful expression. If he had been a dog, his ears might have drooped.

"I'm sorry for pushing you so hard. But I really needed you for today's 'exorcism.' That power of yours, to recognize lies."

"...Why?"

"Because those girls needed the truth," Takatsuki said.

He continued.

"Their curse came from not being able to tell each other the truth. So they needed the truth forced upon them... Somehow, I was able to guess what was happening to the two of them, but it was still just a guess. It wasn't fact. I can be ignorant about other people's feelings, and I couldn't be sure I wouldn't make an error in that situation. I knew that even if I proceeded with the story, if my assumptions were incorrect, those girls would never open up."

That's why he had chosen his words while looking at Ayane's and Kotoko's reactions and comparing them to how Naoya responded to that. So he could confirm and reinforce his guesses.

"But I didn't realize lie detecting would be such a burden on you... Hey, Fukamachi, I'm sorry if I'm wrong, but I think it's about time I know the truth about you, too."

He leaned toward Naoya just a little.

"In actuality, you... It's not people's mannerisms or words, is it? You can tell when someone is lying just from hearing their voice, right?"

Ah, Naoya thought, hearing that, *I've been found out.*

He must have been exposed ages ago. There was no way this perceptive man hadn't figured it out.

So Naoya gave a small nod.

"I see; so that was it," Takatsuki muttered.

"How does it work? Hearing the lies, I mean," he asked.

"The voice sounds…warped. Like some chaotic sound filter has been put over it. That's why it feels awful to listen to."

"I see. But you weren't born like this, were you? Something must have triggered it. Or so I assume."

Takatsuki's tone as he questioned Naoya was soft, gentle, and kind. His concern was clear in his voice.

Naoya went silent for a moment.

He could feel something rising in his throat. Something painful and warm blocking up his throat and chest. He knew he was about to cry. It was all the fault of Takatsuki's gentle voice. He wanted to entrust everything to that voice.

"The night of the festival, when I was ten."

When he opened his mouth, the words poured out automatically.

It was like blood starting to pour from a wound, and there was no longer anything Naoya could do to stop it.

"The one I wrote about in my report. That festival. It all started then."

"Yes, I'm listening. Tell me everything."

Takatsuki nodded.

Naoya spoke. About the day he couldn't go to the festival because he had a fever. About hearing the thundering of the drums in the middle of the night. About running alone to the festival grounds where everyone was dancing.

Everything, even what he hadn't written in his report.

"When I was watching the festival dance, someone grabbed me by the shoulder. When I turned around, I saw a man in a fire-breathing jester mask… He said, '…What are you doing here?' and 'You shouldn't be here…' It was…my grandfather's voice."

It was his grandfather.

Even with his face covered by a mask, Naoya had known right away.

The grandfather he loved so much.

"My grandfather had died the year before that."

It was exactly as Takatsuki had said. That festival was for the dead.

The attendees were likely all spirits of the deceased. Even though Naoya was alive, he had slipped in among them. Even though he shouldn't have.

That's why he was made to pay a price.

Most likely, if he hadn't paid, he wouldn't have been allowed to leave.

"I was taken to a stall and told to choose a sweet. There was a candied apple, a candied plum, and an amber-colored lollipop."

Then his grandfather had told him—

If you choose the apple, you won't be able to walk.

If you choose the plum, you'll lose your words.

And if you choose the lollipop—

"'If you choose the lollipop, you will be lonely.' That's what my grandfather said."

"Lonely...?"

"Yes. I didn't really understand what he meant. I thought 'loneliness' meant no more than being by oneself. That's why I chose the lollipop right away. I was afraid of not being able to walk or talk. I had to eat the lollipop right then and there. I don't remember anything after that. When I woke up, I was back in my futon."

From that point on, all lies sounded incredibly warped to Naoya.

Maybe if he had picked a different sweet, he would have developed some other power. Instead of being unable to walk or talk, a different ability may have come forth.

But there was no way it would have been something good.

Because his ability was a punishment for his crime. The crime of trespassing in the festival of the dead as a living person.

That kind of price couldn't be something insignificant.

"People lie so much. And they hate it when you point that out... I was still a kid... I didn't really understand that. When I noticed someone lying, I would say, 'You just told a lie.'"

None of the people whose lies he exposed were understanding.

Instead, they would scold him, saying, "Don't be ridiculous." Some of them would even turn it around on him and say he was the one who was lying.

And as time went on, gradually, everyone distanced themselves from Naoya. "You give me the creeps," they would hurl at him.

He stopped liking sweet things after that. Every time he recalled the sweet flavor of that amber-colored lollipop melting over his tongue, he was hit with a rush of regret. Countless times he wished he had not gone to that festival.

"The worst incident was with my parents... When I was a first-year in middle school, my father was having an affair. He would say he was going on a business trip, but he would really be meeting up with another woman. I think my mother had known for a while, although she never openly accused him. Then one day, when my father said, 'I'm leaving for a business trip tomorrow'...without thinking, I said, 'Liar.'"

Naoya would never forget the looks on his parents' faces at that moment.

Their eyes opened wide, their faces stiff and twisted as they stared at him.

At that moment, they knew, too. They knew Naoya could hear when someone was lying.

With a single word, Naoya had made his father's affair, which his mother had been pretending she didn't see, into something real. He destroyed his father's lie in an instant.

"...It's not like they got divorced or anything like that after. Their relationship was a mess for a while, though. At least they managed to maintain the appearance of being a family... But—"

The words stuck in his throat. Naoya took another drink from the plastic bottle.

Takatsuki was listening intently.

Naoya continued.

"But instead, both of them stopped speaking in front of me...almost entirely."

Their son who could expose any lie.

He wondered what his parents felt when they realized that.

If they told a lie, their son would cover his ears in disgust. With that, whoever they were talking to would also know they were lying.

Everything would've been fine if they just didn't tell lies. There would've been no problem.

But human beings are liars. They spew lies without even really being conscious of it.

Living without lying was difficult—so there was no choice but to speak as little as possible in front of their son, who could tell when they were lying.

That's probably what his parents had thought.

That was why Naoya wanted to leave his parents' house as soon as he could. No wonder his parents let him move out without a fuss. With a son like him in the house, how could they feel at ease?

"I get it now, what my grandfather meant when he said I would be lonely. No one wants to be around me knowing I can tell when they're lying. Not even my parents."

If that's how things were going to be, Naoya thought he would be better by himself.

He listened to music so he wouldn't have to hear anything unpleasant. Wore glasses to keep the world on the other side of his glass field of vision. Built a wall around himself that said Do Not Enter. Allowed no one else to come inside and, in return, didn't let himself leave, either.

"I also don't—*especially* don't—want to hear the voice of a liar. I don't want to be around someone who lies. It's awful, having to keep hearing those distorted voices... Having someone whose lies I exposed look at me as if I were a monster, it's..."

If you choose that one, you will be lonely.

That was how it was. That was exactly how things had turned out.

His vision blurred, and Naoya wiped at the corners of his eyes roughly. *Pathetic.* A college student on the verge of tears. But he couldn't stop.

It was the first time he had ever told anyone the whole story.

He had probably always wanted to talk about it.

Wanted someone to listen so badly he could barely stand it.

Someone who would take him seriously. Someone who would believe him.

"Here, a handkerchief. It's damp, but use it."

Takatsuki spoke up.

At the same time, a large hand patted Naoya on the head.

"Thank you for telling me... I'm glad I was finally able to hear your story."

Naoya dabbed at his tears with the handkerchief that had been on his forehead only a short while ago. He still couldn't stop crying.

"I don't have ears that can hear lies like yours do, Fukamachi... But I think everything you told me was the truth. I believe you."

His voice was clear and undistorted.

"I've been wondering about you for a while. You're alone most of the time. I noticed you in class and around campus. I wondered at first if you couldn't be bothered with others—or didn't like people in general. But when I actually spoke to you, you were unexpectedly kind. Caring, too. But I got the feeling you were deliberately taking care to get involved with others as little as possible. So...this is the reason."

His large hand gently stroked Naoya's head.

I'm not a child; you don't have to do that, Naoya thought. But even so, for some reason, it didn't occur to him to brush the hand away.

"Fukamachi, if it bothers you, I swear I will never lie in front of you. So can I ask you for one thing in exchange?"

"...What is it?"

"I want you to stay by my side from now on."

Naoya looked up at him. He blinked slowly, staring at Takatsuki.

Eyes the color of the night sky were calmly looking back at him. A genuine night sky, one that Naoya thought he could even see the twinkling of stars in, if only he looked hard enough. Deep, alluring, endless night.

Who was this man, really? Questions sprang up in his chest, completely out of place.

What did the world look like, reflected in those eyes that held the night? *What do I look like to him?* Naoya wondered.

"...Doesn't it disgust you? What I can do."

He repeated the question he had asked once before.

With a small *pfft*, a smile appeared on Takatsuki's lips.

It was a rueful smile, completely different from the bright one he usually wore.

"If someone is disgusted by you, I'm sure they would be disgusted by me as well, you know."

"Huh...?"

Before Naoya could ask what that meant, Takatsuki spoke again.

"Hey, Fukamachi. Someday, let's figure out what happened to you. Together!"

His tone was back to being excited and full of curiosity. His eyes returned to being brown, and his smile shone once more like a clear, sunny day.

As he spoke, he leaned toward Naoya, swinging his legs back and forth like a child.

"I don't know if your ears will ever return to normal, but let's find out what that festival you went to really was. For that reason also, I definitely want you to stay by my side! Is that okay? It's okay, right?"

Momentarily taken aback, Naoya blinked again. A tear that had clung to one of his eyelashes fell at last.

Ah, he really is this kind of person, Naoya thought.

He didn't know him well at all, but... Even so, that golden-retriever-like smile—Takatsuki's smiling face, which Naoya was so acquainted with—there was no mistaking it.

"...If you go to that festival, you'll have to pay the price, too, Professor."

Takatsuki replied, his smile crinkling at the corners.

"That's fine. If it happens, I'll choose something different than you did."

"It would be better if you didn't choose one at all, though."

A smile surfaced on Naoya's face as well. He had a feeling that Takatsuki really would be able to figure it out someday. He'd uncover the truth of everything that happened that night.

Naoya grabbed his glasses from the table and put them on. He thought about returning the handkerchief to Takatsuki but decided to hold off.

"Um... I'll wash this and return it."

"Oh, it's fine. You don't have to do that."

Takatsuki held out his hand, but Naoya put the handkerchief in his pocket. He was pretty sure he had also gotten snot on it while he was wiping his tears.

"But I guess I can't use you as a lie detector anymore, can I? I didn't know it would be that painful. I made a mistake there; I'm sorry."

"...No, it's fine; I'm not mad. I'll be okay if it's only every now and then."

As he replied, Naoya realized the materials Takatsuki had prepared were still on the table. The girls hadn't taken the papers with them. Well, he hadn't really expected them to anyway.

"...What will those two do from now on?"

Hearing Naoya murmur while he was picking up the materials, Takatsuki turned to look over his shoulder.

"What do you mean?"

"I mean, they were just lying back and forth to each other. Even a statement like 'We'll always, always be friends...' was a lie. I wonder if they really can keep being friends from now on."

"Well now...who can say?"

Takatsuki made a neat stack of the papers he had gathered.

"They may well be able to continue getting along just fine like that, surprisingly enough. Women are generally more complex than you or I.

Even if things don't go as perfectly as they have until now, they might be able to be fairly close as friends."

"Do you really think so?"

"Yep. At the very least, they still had enough heart to worry about each other."

"Even though they lied?"

"*Because* they lied."

Naoya's head cocked to the side in confusion. He didn't really understand what his professor was saying.

Takatsuki slid the papers between folders on his shelves.

"You know, Fukamachi... I think there's such a thing as a necessary lie."

"A necessary lie?"

"Yes. A lie told for the other person's sake."

Takatsuki smiled broadly.

"For example, let's say a mother with a small child catches a cold. She has a fever and feels awful. Naturally, her child will anxiously ask her, 'Mama, are you okay?' The mother in that situation would probably answer, 'I'm fine.' Even if her fever is actually over a hundred, and she's not fine at all, she wouldn't want to make her child worry."

Surely that wasn't true. It wouldn't really happen.

But he understood what Takatsuki was saying, more or less.

"I think it's the same with those two. They could have ended things by hurling insults at each other. But if they had, they would have hurt themselves as well as each other. To keep things as peaceful as possible and to avoid hurting one another, they deliberately lied."

That was Takatsuki's interpretation.

After hearing that everything the girls had said then was a lie, this rationalization of Takatsuki's was the result. Whether it was true, Naoya didn't know.

But, he thought, it wasn't a bad way to interpret things.

Takatsuki had told him before that the important thing was how one interpreted a phenomenon. If that was true, it might not hurt to try believing in Takatsuki's interpretation.

It felt a lot better than the alternative: believing that the two of them came to the worst conclusion after leaving.

"Fukamachi. I have to attend to something at the registrar's office for a little while, but please rest here a bit longer. When you feel better, feel free to go home. Don't worry about locking up. I'll do it later."

That said, Takatsuki left Naoya in his office and went out.

He was feeling a lot better, but Naoya appreciated the invitation to keep resting, so he decided to do that. Takatsuki's lab, with its used-bookstore smell, was comfortable and quiet.

He lay back down on the makeshift folding chair couch and closed his eyes.

For a little while, he slept.

He woke with a start to the sound of the door clanging open. Confused, he sat up.

He wondered if Takatsuki had come back, but it was Ruiko who was looking back at him. She had her glasses on today, instead of contacts.

"Oh, Fukamachi, you're here? What's wrong? Are you sick?"

"...Yeah, sort of... I was dizzy. Professor Takatsuki told me to rest."

"I see. I'm sorry, did I wake you up? Professor Akira said that case with the two girls would be settled today, and I was curious, so I came. It's already over, isn't it?"

"Yeah."

"How did it turn out? Was it a knockdown, drag-out deal?"

"No, I feel like things ended peacefully...I guess."

"Is that so? Well, I thought it might go in that direction, you know. Professor Akira is a kind person, after all."

Ruiko turned to face the bookshelves. She ran her finger along the spines of the books and pulled out a few. Apparently, she had also come to borrow materials.

Naoya nodded in response to her statement.

"He really is a kind person... Professor Takatsuki, I mean."

He had a feeling there had been a high chance of things ending differently between Ayane and Kotoko. The girls had ended up worrying about one another, even if they were lying, but it wouldn't have been unexpected if, as Ruiko had said, things had devolved into a fistfight. Takatsuki had chosen his words carefully and guided the two of them to avoid that outcome. He pointed out that Ayane had protected Kotoko and said they were both feeling cornered.

Naoya wondered if he himself had been helpful to Takatsuki.

In the end, he had collapsed, but even so, if Takatsuki was able to successfully make use of his ability for his "exorcism," then, well. That was something to be happy about, just a little.

Because it seemed as though his ears, which had only ever caused him grief, could be used for something good.

"Absolutely, Professor Akira is so kind. He's like an angel... Or rather, he might actually *be* an angel."

Ruiko murmured those words in earnest, with the books she had picked out clutched to her chest.

Naoya almost burst into laughter.

"What, an angel...? Miss Ruiko, you're surprisingly romantic, aren't you?"

"I am not! I didn't mean it like that, I just—I mean, I saw it, once."

"Huh? Saw what? Not wings, right?"

Naoya smiled sarcastically. Ruiko started to reply, then closed her mouth.

She looked around, then even stuck her head out the door to make sure no one was in the hallway before coming back.

Just as Takatsuki had done a short while before, she perched on the edge of the table. Pushing up her glasses, she spoke as if she were about to reveal the world's biggest secret.

"...Listen. This absolutely cannot leave this room."

"Wh-what is it?"

"Once...I saw Professor Akira's back."

"H-his back? When would you have seen that?"

"I-it's not like I was undressing him or anything! We went to a research seminar together last year and got caught in a downpour!"

Ruiko had turned bright red. She might really be a secret romantic.

"Neither of us had an umbrella, and we got soaked. And it was summer, so I wasn't wearing anything over my blouse, and it became see-through... Professor Akira noticed right away. He took off his own jacket and let me wear it. Because he's a *gentleman!*"

The rain had come down hard that day, and Takatsuki's white button-down was soaked through. Enough for his skin to be visible through his wet shirt.

That's when Ruiko saw it, she said. Saw them.

Two huge scars on Takatsuki's back.

Scars spread wide over both sides of his broad back, starting at his shoulder blades and ending near his hip bones.

"It was like he had...wings, but they got ripped off."

That's why, Ruiko said, with an earnest expression, Takatsuki might be an angel who fell from the sky.

Chapter 3:
The House to Another World

Summer break ended, and the students returned to campus.

Although, as should probably be expected of college students, there were also those brave students who continued traveling abroad for the whole of September. All the first classes that took place after summer break were sparsely attended, and those who did show up were still looking fairly sluggish from vacation.

Takatsuki's class was no exception. As he looked around the half-empty lecture hall, the professor smiled lightly.

"Ah, not everyone is back from their great summer adventure yet, I see... Well, it's the same way every year. Since there aren't many of you today, I'm not going to split this topic into two lectures. We'll just wrap it up for today. Today's theme, to put it plainly, is 'kamikakushi'! Now, for the materials."

Naoya took the occasion to quickly scan the classroom as he passed the materials to the students behind him and spotted Ayane and Kotoko. They were sitting side by side, so it seemed like they were still friends.

Once he had confirmed that the materials had made it all the way to the back of the room, Takatsuki continued talking.

"Kamikakushi literally means 'to be hidden by the gods,' and it points to instances when, one day, out of the blue, someone or something is just gone. Spirited away. To put it another way, it's when someone is lost or goes missing. In the past, people thought such things were the work of gods. 'Someone who should definitely be here has vanished; that's strange—surely the gods have hidden them away.' That kind of feeling. In particular, children went missing frequently in the past. Kidnapping cases still happen a lot today, but it happened in greater numbers back then. And that was also thought to be the work of gods or monsters. For example, Figure 1 in the handout."

The diagram Takatsuki had mentioned was a picture that looked like the indecipherable doodle of a child. Whatever it was, its head and body were the same size, and its black hair was so long that it dragged on the ground. Its long nose looked like a wooden rod that had been glued to its face, and its distinctive mouth opened all the way to the ears. Takatsuki told the class that the monster wasn't one of his own drawings, but one that had come from *Mikikigusa*.

"From the summer of the first year of the Tenmei era until the following year, this monster is said to have carried off many boys and girls under the age of fifteen, from a wide area that spanned from what is today Fukushima prefecture, all the way to modern-day Akita prefecture. Ultimately, the monster was shot dead by a hunter, but its true nature is unclear. But this terribly long nose—I wonder if it reminds anyone of a very widely known mythical creature…? That's right, it looks like a *tengu*, doesn't it? There are actually tons of stories of *tengu* carrying people off."

Takatsuki continued.

"As cited in Handout 2, in the essay '*Shozan Chomon Kishu*,' a story is mentioned in which a boy in the former Mino province was carried away by a *tengu* while he was taking a bath. In '*Gaidan Bunbun Shuyo*,' mentioned in Handout 3, there's a story of a young man being kidnapped by a *tengu* and carried from Kyoto to Edo. The story happened around eight o'clock at night, on the twentieth of July in 1810. A man was found standing, buck naked, in a daze, on Umamichi Street in Asakusa."

The phrase *buck naked* had quite the impact on the classroom. Laughter and muttering mixed in the air.

With a smile, Takatsuki continued talking.

"The man was a twenty-five-year-old from Kyoto named Yasujirou. Two days prior, Yasujirou had made a pilgrimage to Mount Atago in Kyoto, and an old monk told him he would show Yasujirou something interesting. I think even today we're often told from childhood that we shouldn't go with strangers, but Yasujirou followed the old monk. He had no memory of what happened afterward. When he came to, he was standing in Asakusa, not even wearing a loincloth. So why did the people of the time think this incident was the work of a *tengu*? Actually, Yasujirou wasn't completely naked. He was wearing nothing but his split-toe socks. Those socks had absolutely no mud on them. In that era, it was virtually impossible to travel from Kyoto to Edo in two days, and on top of that, because his feet were clean, people believed he must have flown in the sky. Because *tengu* have wings, you see. This young man was definitely picked up by a *tengu* and flown through the sky to get here—that's how people at the time interpreted it."

Takatsuki's smoothly flowing voice was as gentle as ever, resounding pleasantly around the room.

The first classes post-vacation also tended to be full of students dozing off, but most of the ones in Takatsuki's class seemed to be listening attentively. Well, it was a strange story about being kidnapped by a *tengu*, so it was just more fun to listen to than overly scholarly topics.

"Now, even so, is anyone wondering why *tengu* are so linked to disappearance cases? *Tengu* are a fairly large part of Japanese folklore, aren't they? In addition to the one at Mount Atago mentioned in the story, the *tengu* at Mount Kurama in Kyoto are also famous. And it seems that people back in the day believed that the *tengu* had their own world. The world of the *tengu*—in other words, the spirit world. A place slightly different from the world of the living. They believed that's where people went when they were carried off. They also believed there were children who could travel between the two worlds at will, who would go to the *tengu* world to gain knowledge of it to bring back. A young boy named Torakichi, who appears in Handouts 4 and 5, 'Heiji Daito' by Yoshishige Yamazaki and 'Senkyo Ibun' by Hirata Atsutane, was said to be one such child. Torakichi served as an errand boy for the *tengu* that had taken him away for several years. He demonstrated the knowledge he had gained in the *tengu* world and answered various questions about it. He covered a wide range of topics, including Shinto and Buddhist fables, stories about the world of the *tengu*, how to treat illnesses, and so on. He was asked some odd questions as well, such as why it was bad to pluck long nose hairs, and if he could give detailed recipes of the dishes his *tengu* master had made. It's quite entertaining, so I really recommend reading those books if you have time."

Turning away from the class, Takatsuki started to write on the blackboard. Dressed in his suit jacket, straight-backed, his arm outstretched as he wrote.

Looking at Takatsuki's back, Naoya remembered Ruiko's words from several days before.

Takatsuki had two huge scars on his back.

Like he'd had his wings clipped.

Maybe Ruiko, who thought Takatsuki was an angel because of those scars, was a bit of a romantic. For starters, if he'd had his wings clipped and fell from the heavens, wouldn't that make him a *fallen* angel? Wouldn't that make him a demon?

Even entertaining the topic to that point, Naoya felt foolish. Naturally, Takatsuki wasn't a demon.

The professor was carrying on his lecture from the dais, smiling as he carried on. He looked nothing more than human, of course, and Naoya expected that he was only human, in reality. Sure, he had a somewhat otherworldly atmosphere about him.

But then—what was it Takatsuki had told him before?

When Naoya had asked him if his ability to hear lies—the price he had paid for going to the festival of the dead—was disgusting to Takatsuki.

Right.

He had said, "If someone is disgusted by you, I'm sure they would be disgusted by me as well, you know."

What did that mean?

Summer break came to a close, and classes started back up before Naoya had the chance to ask.

Takatsuki conducted the lecture just as he had in the previous semester, putting the chalk down right as the bell rang to signal the end of class.

"Well, that's all for today. Next week, we'll cover a different topic. See you then."

In the end, the *kamikakushi* topic had progressed into *tengu* fables and kidnapping stories—and even into modern missing persons cases. As always, Takatsuki jumped casually between subjects—from how children were often kidnapped in the past to secure labor forces, to stories of *tengu* carrying off pretty young boys to keep as their own—but still somehow managed, more or less, to tie everything together by the end. It was amazing.

Gathering up his things and heading out of the lecture hall, Naoya thought of going to the library, then felt his phone vibrate in his pocket.

Taking it out, he saw a message from Takatsuki. *"I have some work for you, so please come to my office if you're free."*

Thinking that this semester seemed to be heading in much the same direction as the last, Naoya set a course for Takatsuki's office instead of the library.

When he arrived at the office, he saw on the table a number of confectionery boxes that looked like souvenirs.

"What are these?"

At Naoya's question, Takatsuki beamed. He was in the middle of unwrapping a sweet red bean wafer.

"Since this morning, each of my graduate students has been bringing me souvenirs from summer vacation! Since everyone knows I love sugary things, I've gotten a ton of sweets!"

He happily stuffed the wafer into his mouth. He really didn't look anything like a fallen angel.

There were five boxes of sweets on the table. His graduate students really adored him, to bring him that many. The mug Takatsuki had put on the table seemed to contain roasted green tea today, instead of his usual cocoa.

"Do you want some coffee, Fukamachi? I have rice crackers over there; feel free to eat some."

Takatsuki stood and went to the coffee maker. There was indeed a package of rice crackers alongside the sweets boxes.

"Oh, that's right. Bring your own personal cup with you next time, okay?"

"Huh?"

"Unless you just want the Great Buddha cup to be yours? If you like it that much, I'd be happy to give it to you."

Takatsuki held up the colorful Great Buddha mug he always used for Naoya's coffee.

"No, I really don't like it… I just don't care about having a personal cup."

"What? But I mean—you come here all the time. And you're going to major in folklore studies as well, right?"

"I haven't decided yet."

"What?"

Naoya really wished Takatsuki wouldn't look at him like that, with all that genuine surprise on his face.

"F-Fukamachi? Aren't you going to major in folklore studies and be one of my graduate students?"

"Like I said, I haven't decided yet. I said that to Miss Ruiko recently, too, you know."

"Is…is that so…? Hmm… Well, I don't care if you major in English literature or Japanese history, as long as you work with me…"

Takatsuki grumbled to himself as he poured Naoya's coffee. Apparently, just like Ruiko, the professor had assumed from the beginning that Naoya would be joining his research group.

Taking the coffee cup, Naoya looked at Takatsuki again.

"So what's the job today?"

"Oh, right. Well, I got this request. It feels timely, as it relates to today's lecture."

Takatsuki opened his laptop and showed it to Naoya.

"It's from a second-year high school girl who lives in Chofu. She said her friend has been spirited away. I'm thinking of going to meet her and listen to her story. Do you want to come with me, Fukamachi?"

"Ah... Sure. I'll go."

Naoya accepted the invitation, thinking how odd it was that such bizarre incidents happened even in modern times.

The high school girl who had emailed Takatsuki was called Hana Mizutani.

They met her at a café in front of Chofu Station in the early afternoon on Sunday. When she spotted Takatsuki, she waved quickly at him. She had long brown hair, was wearing light makeup, and looked like an average modern high school girl.

As Takatsuki and Naoya sat down across from her, Hana stared at Takatsuki for a minute, happily kicking her feet.

"H-h-hi, I'm Hana Mizutani, the person who emailed you! *Wow*, you are, like, so handsome, *omigosh*! Can I, like, take a picture of you?"

"Hello, I'm Takatsuki, from Seiwa University. This is my student, Fukamachi. Thank you, but no pictures, please."

Hana had lifted her smartphone as she asked for the photo, but Takatsuki gently rebuffed her.

She frowned a little.

"Why nooot? I won't post it to, like, Insta or anything."

"Well, because some people may find it suspicious that a college professor is talking to a high school girl. I'm here today to consult with you about the serious matter in your email. That's why it's inappropriate to do things like that—things you would normally do with friends."

"*Geez*... You're no fun..."

Hana started to pout, but when Takatsuki smiled at her, she quickly brightened up and put away her phone. Handsome men sure did have it easy in some ways, Naoya thought. They could improve someone else's mood like magic with a single smile.

Once Takatsuki and Naoya had ordered, Hana went back to staring at the professor, this time while stirring her own iced tea with a straw.

"Hey, sooo…do you really believe what I said in my email?"

"If I didn't, I wouldn't have come all the way here," Takatsuki replied.

"Well, I won't really know until I hear the story in detail. But at the very least, I thought your story didn't seem like a prank, so I decided to come and hear it in person."

"Huh… I thought adults might not take this kind of thing seriously."

"Ah, well, I'm often told that I have the body and mind of an adult but the heart of a child, so."

"What's with that?"

Hana snorted and burst into giggles.

Then her expression changed slightly, and she sat up straight.

Until this point, meeting the two of them face-to-face for the first time, she must have been a little nervous. Dropping her easygoing act, Hana looked at them with a serious face.

"…So. My friend was spirited away at the end of summer vacation."

The friend was someone she knew from school, Hana told them. Their classes were different, but they were both in the school band. The girl's name was Sayuki Matsuno.

"Oh, I should tell you first: Sayuki has been found already. She was only missing for two days. But…the way she went missing, it was weird."

With that preface, Hana began to tell her story.

"My school has a ton of club activities even during summer break. I was also taking a short class for summer term at a cram school. I didn't have a lot of free time. But I kept telling Sayuki, since it was summer break and all, that I wanted to do something memorable. But the sea is far away, and pools are crowded, so when I asked Sayuki what we should do, she said…'Let's do something scary.'"

Hana had thought her friend was talking about going to a haunted house or something. There were a lot of amusement parks that put on especially elaborate haunted houses as a part of their limited-time summer programming.

But that wasn't what Sayuki had meant.

"'No, not that, something more real. Something that doesn't cost money.' That's what she said. I was like, 'What on earth is she talking about?' so I asked, and she said there was a deserted house in the mountains near her home. People say it's haunted, and she was talking about sneaking in there in the middle of the night."

"Ah, that's a very innocent way of having an adventure. Although, it would be trespassing."

Takatsuki smiled wryly.

Hana frowned a little, crossed her arms, and sat back hard in her seat. "That's what I said! I was like, 'That's a crime!'"

But Sayuki didn't back down.

She laughed and said, "It's fine; let's do it." According to her, there were other kids in the neighborhood near her home who had tested their courage in that house.

Even so, Hana was uncomfortable with the idea, and before long, Sayuki had told her, "I get it, I get it. You're scared; I'm not going to force you to do it." And "It's fine; I'll just do it by myself."

"…I should have tried harder to stop her then."

Hana's voice started to tremble all of a sudden.

Regret plain on her face and in her voice, she continued speaking in a faint voice.

"But I didn't. I told her, 'Yeah, fine, go by yourself, then! I want to make sure you actually do it, so you better take pictures—or a video or whatever!' I… I egged her on."

"So did Miss Sayuki go to the deserted house alone?"

Hana gave a small nod in response to Takatsuki's question.

Then Sayuki disappeared.

Sayuki had told Hana to stay awake because she was going to do a live stream from the house on LINE. But that night, other than a message that said "*I'm heading out now,*" Hana wasn't contacted by her friend at all. Hana had assumed Sayuki had merely decided not to go after all because she had realized it was a dumb idea.

But the next morning, she learned Sayuki was missing. One of Hana's friends from her club activities, who was in the same class as Sayuki, had received a LINE message from Sayuki's parents that said "*Our daughter didn't come home last night. Do you know anything?*" The night before, Sayuki had told her parents she was going to the convenience store when she left the house, and she hadn't come back.

Hana had considered telling Sayuki's parents that their daughter was out doing a silly dare. But right as she was about to contact them, she hesitated.

"Because I thought, what if right after I tell them, she turns up safe and sound but gets scolded for doing something stupid? I wasn't sure what to do…"

"Hmm, that might not have been the right call. In that kind of situation, it's better to tell an adult right away, don't you think?"

"Well, I had a lot to think about in the moment! …So I decided to go check the abandoned house before telling her parents. I thought maybe Sayuki had collapsed in there or something…"

"Don't tell me you went by yourself?"

"Yeah… I mean, during the day, obviously. I thought maybe it wouldn't be scary if it was light out."

She had learned the approximate location of the house from Sayuki.

She went looking and found a house that seemed to be the right place. The house appeared extremely dilapidated. Hana was terrified, so much so that she thought about just turning back. But when she remembered that Sayuki may be inside, she couldn't just give up on her.

She thought the neighborhood would be empty enough that she could peek inside the house without being questioned by anyone.

She decided to at least start by scouting out the house's interior from inside the yard, and so she reached for the front gate.

Then suddenly, from behind her, someone asked, "Can I help you?" She turned around to find a man in black tracksuit standing there, holding a convenience store bag.

Certain that no one lived in the house, Hana had been so surprised she almost leaped into the air. She bowed her head and apologized in a hurry, but the man just stood there staring at Hana with a very wary look on his face.

So Hana had said, "Actually, my friend went missing around here. Do you happen to know anything about that?"

Head cocked to the side, the man had replied, "I hadn't heard anything about that." Sayuki's disappearance hadn't been reported, so it made sense that he didn't know about it.

But his next words were baffling.

"He was like, 'But I heard from an older lady who passed away that people often get spirited away around here, so you better be careful, too. If your friend got carried off by something, she'll turn up somewhere sooner or later, so don't worry.'"

And just as the man had said, they found Sayuki unharmed the very next night.

The person who found her reported that she was lying in the street in Hachiōji, far from where she lived.

At the time, she was only vaguely conscious, so they took her to the hospital right away. She had no physical trauma in particular, but her memory was vague, and she couldn't even remember where she had been while she was missing. When she was discharged from the hospital, Hana asked her if she had gone to the deserted house as planned, but Sayuki didn't even remember that much. Sayuki's parents suspected their daughter had been forced to drink alcohol or something similar, but nothing was detected in the hospital's tests.

Hana couldn't help but think her friend had been spirited away, since she had both disappeared and reappeared abruptly. Even Hana's parents, when they heard the story, said, "It's just like *kamikakushi*, isn't it?"

"Since Sayuki has already come home safely, maybe there's no need to dig into things now. But I can't help worrying about it."

Hana fixed her gaze on Takatsuki.

"Hey, Professor. Is *kamikakushi* real? What happens to someone while they're missing? Do they get hurt? Do they suffer? Is it possible to find out what happened to Sayuki while she was gone? If it is, please, please find out!"

"...Well, before that, can I say something first?"

Hana's words were pouring out in a rush, and Takatsuki held up a hand slightly to stop her.

Hana snapped her mouth shut and blinked.

"What is it?"

"Well. It's not your fault that Miss Sayuki disappeared, you know."

Takatsuki's voice was soft. He looked at Hana dead-on.

Hana's shoulders jolted.

Long eyelashes trembling, she looked off a little, trying to escape from Takatsuki's gaze. When she opened her mouth again, her voice shook in utter dismay.

"...B-but I...I should have stopped her. If I had... If I had, then Sayuki—"

"When Miss Sayuki suggested going into the house, you rightly told her it was a bad idea. She was the one who ignored you and went alone. Maybe there was an element of friends stubbornly competing with one another that made it hard for her to back down, but that's not something you should feel responsible for," Takatsuki said, his voice all gentle reason.

On top of the table, both of Hana's hands balled up into fists.

Her face was crumpled, like she was barely seconds away from crying. Just before the tears gathered in her eyes began to fall, she hung her head. The tears pattered onto the table, making splotches on the surface.

She really does think it's her fault, Naoya thought, watching her.

To the point that she took the trouble to go to Takatsuki for help.

Even if the incident itself was settled, in Hana's mind, nothing had been resolved yet, it seemed.

"Now then, I certainly am interested in finding out what happened to Miss Sayuki. I don't know yet whether she was spirited away, but I will try to investigate."

Hana dabbed at her eyes with a handkerchief and looked up at Takatsuki.

"You'll help…? Really?"

"Yep. I'm extremely interested in *kamikakushi*, so if this case really is one, well."

Takatsuki smiled broadly.

Seeing that expression, Naoya recalled a feeling of vague discomfort.

This was usually around the time in consultations where Takatsuki went into "Senselessness Mode." It wouldn't be out of place for him to hug Hana and start prattling on at a near shout about how excited he was. Putting a stop to that was why Naoya, the Sensible One, was sitting at Takatsuki's side.

But this time, things weren't going like that.

Usually when Takatsuki's interest wasn't piqued, it was because he knew from the start that nothing supernatural was involved. But if that was the case here, then what reason was there to accept Hana's request?

Naoya glanced sidelong at Takatsuki, wondering what it all meant.

Still looking at Hana, Takatsuki spoke up again.

"Speaking of, I'm guessing the reason Miss Sayuki isn't sitting here with you now is because you haven't told her you asked me for help. Or maybe you did, and she asked you not to?"

"Oh…I didn't tell her. About consulting you or anything."

"Why?"

"If Sayuki herself forgot, I feel like maybe it's better not to force her to remember. One time I went to her house to ask her a few things about it, but her mom stopped me before I could. She told me, 'Sayuki might have forgotten out of shock, so just let it be.' That's why… Asking you for help, it's totally for my own benefit… Is that wrong?"

Hana's brow sank, as though her confidence was capsizing, too.

Takatsuki shook his head.

"It's not wrong. It just means I won't be able to talk to Miss Sayuki herself... Do you know anything else about her disappearance or discovery? If you do, please tell me everything."

"Um, I mean, I've already told you everything... Oh yeah," she said, looking like something had just come to mind.

"Someone was living in that old house, so it might not have anything to do with Sayuki's disappearance. But I think wherever she was while she was missing, it must have been indoors."

"Why do you think that?"

"Because when they found her, she wasn't wearing shoes," Hana said. "But the soles of her feet weren't dirty at all. Maybe that's unrelated, but just in case, y'know?"

For a moment, it felt like Takatsuki was holding his breath.

When Naoya looked at him, he was staring at the table with a slightly tense expression.

"...Professor? What's wrong?"

At Naoya's question, Takatsuki looked over at him, seeming to snap out of it.

"No, it's nothing. I was just thinking it's like the story in 'Gaidan Bunbun Shuyo,' that's all. You know, the story I told in class last time? Of Yasujirou, who turned up in Asakusa with only one clean sock? It's a bit similar, isn't it?"

Takatsuki smiled as he answered.

But for some reason, that smile seemed terribly sad compared to his usual radiance.

They decided to start by investigating the abandoned house. Well, since someone was living there, maybe it wasn't abandoned, but that's what they chose to call it for the time being.

With Hana guiding them, they took a bus from in front of the station to a stop near Sayuki's house. Even though they were still in Tokyo, this area was pretty verdant and mountainous.

The abandoned house was a short walk from the bus stop. It was built near the middle of a low mountain. The dense, leafy trees looming behind the house made it look like the house itself was about to be engulfed by the mountain. Other houses were sparse in the area, and there was no one walking by.

"Wow. This is quite the 'abandoned house,' isn't it?" Takatsuki said.

It certainly looked the picture of "abandoned." Moss clung to the walls here and there, and the trees and grass in the yard were growing as they pleased. Through the balcony, they could see the second floor's glass door was covered by a silver tarp instead of rain shutters. But because the tarp itself was tattered and half peeled away, the sliding paper shoji door inside was totally visible. The shoji was also so torn to shreds that they could only guess what had caused it.

The faint writing on the wooden door plate said HANEDA. Takatsuki pressed the doorbell, but it was likely broken and didn't seem to produce any sound. When Naoya turned to look at the parking space next to the gate, he saw dead leaves piling up, but no car.

Looking out at the practically haunted-seeming house, Naoya muttered without thinking.

"...Does someone actually live here?"

"Mm, I'm not sure."

Takatsuki's head cocked to the side.

Surveying the building from outside the fence, Takatsuki frowned and pointed at the second floor.

"There, do you see that? That window is broken. There are bird droppings and feathers stuck to the frame. I think some kind of bird is building a nest inside... If someone actually does live here, they must be a really kindhearted person who loves wild animals and wants to coexist with nature."

That kind of person probably didn't exist, Naoya thought.

Hana sounded indignant when she replied.

"But there really was a man here! He said, 'Can I help you?' That probably means he lives here, right?!"

"Ah, I'm not doubting what you said. For the time being, it looks like no one is here, so let's try talking to some people in the area, shall we?"

Takatsuki spared one more glance for the abandoned house, then started back the way they had come.

They found a park nearby, and when they asked the grade school children playing there if they knew anything about the "haunted house," they received an enthusiastic response.

"Oh, I know, I know! That old worn-out house in the middle of the mountain over there, right? There's a monster over there, for real!"

A boy who seemed like the leader of the kid pack answered them, speaking in a bragging tone.

Crouching down to be about eye level with the children, Takatsuki opened his eyes wide.

"Really? Have you seen a monster there, by chance?"

"I haven't, but I know there are people who have! Huh, ain't that right?"

When the leader kid asked his friends, they all nodded vigorously.

Takatsuki leaned forward, wearing his own childlike expression.

"That's amazing! What kind of monster was it? A woman? A man? Something that wasn't human, maybe?"

"I dunno, but I heard it's reeeally scary! And some people saw somethin' that looked like a spirit!"

"A spirit? Was it flying in the air?"

"Nope, it was in that house! They said they saw it through the window! Nobody lives there, so the lights don't come on even at night, but they saw somethin' that was glowing a little moving around inside!"

"Whoa, really? That's scary!"

"Right! But I know an even scarier story. Wanna hear it?"

"I want to, I want to! What kind of story?"

Squatting with his elbows resting on his knees, staring up at the leader kid, Takatsuki's eyes sparkled with excitement.

Naoya and Hana watched from a short distance away as the leader kid began to triumphantly share a scary story about his own school. Hana whispered to Naoya as they looked on.

"…Somehow that professor is really good with little kids. Doesn't he work at a college? He's not really an elementary school teacher, is he? Or a kindergarten teacher?"

"No, well… I think that's why people say he has 'the body and mind of an adult but the heart of a child,' you know?"

"Ah… I get it now."

"Yeah…"

Ultimately, the group of kids took to Takatsuki like moths to a flame. The leader kid even told him, "I'll make you my disciple," but Takatsuki said, "Those big kids over there are calling for me, so I have to go," bid the children good-bye, and returned to Naoya and Hana. It was impressive to see all the children shouting, "Come visit again!" at Takatsuki as he waved and called "Bye-bye" over his shoulder. Naoya felt it was rare for someone to charm children this much when meeting them for the first time.

Well, maybe an adult who looked cool but talked and acted like a kid was something that appealed to them. Takatsuki himself seemed to have a lot of fun, too.

"Whew, I didn't expect it, but I even managed to gather some info about a ghost story from a school around here. Those kids were all so great!"

"…Wait, did you forget why we're here? You didn't, right?"

Hana glared at Takatsuki, who laughed loudly.

"Ha-ha, it's fine; I haven't forgotten! Now then, I'd like to try talking to an adult, too… Oh, that person looks like they might be good. Excuuuse me!"

Smiling, he called out to a woman walking in their direction. She looked like she might be a stay-at-home parent.

In stark contrast to his childish behavior from just before, Takatsuki spoke to the woman in a calm, gentlemanly manner, quickly getting her to open up. Hana gaped at him.

"Hey, what is that guy's deal? Is he a pickup artist? A playboy? Or just a professional interrogator?"

"...He's a professor at my school, so I'd rather go with 'professional interrogator,' as far as that goes."

"I mean, like, adults are crazy, aren't they...?"

"Hana, that's not right. That guy isn't a normal adult, so you don't need to assume adults are usually like that, okay?"

"...You really don't hold back, huh?"

Despite Hana's considerable reluctance, Takatsuki's interviews ended up being largely successful, and he gathered a substantial amount of information about the abandoned house.

The three of them rode the bus for a short while back to the station and decided to get a light meal at a fast-food restaurant while sorting out the information they had gathered.

"First off, it seems like no one lives in that house, after all."

Takatsuki picked up a single French fry as he made his declaration.

"But...!"

When Hana opened her mouth to protest loudly, Takatsuki shoved the French fry into it, silencing her so he could continue.

"To begin with, the testimony from Tomoki, the leader kid at the park: 'Nobody lives there, so the lights don't come on even at night...' In other words, this is a fact that even children know. I also asked an adult after that, and she said, 'There shouldn't be anyone living over there now.' Apparently, an elderly woman lived there by herself up until a few years ago, but she passed away, and no one has lived there since. That woman had a son, but he owns a house far away, so for the time being, that house is abandoned. I was told that the neighborhood association discussed wanting to cut down the tree in the yard because it was growing all the way to the road, but they couldn't get in touch with the house's owner, so it's just being left as is."

"...Then who was the person I saw?"

"I'm not sure. I think you can find out who the current owner is by looking up the registration information on the internet, but...it's possible a person moved in without permission. Although, it's not just people who move into places of their own accord."

This time, Takatsuki laughed while putting a French fry in his own mouth.

Hana frowned.

"What do you mean, 'not just people'?"

"I mean there's a nonzero chance that something not human is living there, right? Demons or ghosts or something. I'm not ready to give up on those dreams just yet."

"Professor, let's be a bit more serious, shall we?"

Takatsuki's eyes had begun to sparkle with excitement, but Naoya quickly reeled him in.

The professor pushed his fries toward Naoya apologetically. Naoya didn't particularly want an apology gift, but whatever.

"Seriously speaking, well, it's quite common for homeless people and criminals to sneak into vacant houses. Tomoki said he heard of people seeing spirits floating in the windows. It could have been people carrying flashlights inside, for example, instead of spirits. No one knew about the *kamikakushi* rumors, either. It was well-known as a haunted house among the children, and Miss Sayuki was aware of it, too. But the form of the monster that Tomoki talked about wasn't concrete in the slightest. Typically, if you're telling a ghost story, you at least state whether the monster is male or female, right? In other words, I think it's best to consider that the house got a reputation for being haunted because of the way it looks. It's not uncommon for a thought like *That house is old and scary* to evolve into *There must be a monster in there* and ultimately become *People have seen monsters there*, without any basis at all."

"Then... Then what about Sayuki? What happened to her?"

"The truth is: I still don't know. But I came this far, and I do want to figure it out."

Listening to Takatsuki as he ate his hamburger, Naoya had an awful hunch.

"Professor. It's fine to want to know, but how do you plan to find out?"

"Well, there's nothing else to do but go inside that house."

Takatsuki answered casually, face placid.

Naoya was shocked.

"You said yourself that's a bad idea! It's trespassing!"

"Only if I get caught."

"If you get caught? I can't believe you…"

"Come on; don't you think the only way to the truth is in that house?"

Takatsuki leaned toward Naoya, the corners of his mouth turned upward. He was too close. His sense of personal space was so weird.

"Nothing ventured, nothing gained. That's an old adage, you know. If you aren't prepared to take some risks, you won't get what you want… What? It's fine! If push comes to shove, I've got a guy on the force!"

"Is that how you treat Mr. Sasakura? How awful."

"It's my policy to utilize anything that can be useful."

Naoya started to feel bad for Sasakura. He had probably been used like this before, by his leech of a childhood friend.

Hana shook her head frantically.

"Hey, you don't have to go that far; it would be bad if you got caught, right?"

"It's fine, I said. I'll make sure I don't get caught, and even if I do, I have tricks up my sleeve… Now then, that's all for you today, Miss Hana. You too, Fukamachi. I'll be going into that house alone, so you two head home after you've eaten."

"What? No way!"

"No, I'm going with you!"

Takatsuki smiled in response to Hana's and Naoya's raised voices.

"Nope. There's no way I can invite young people with promising futures to join me in a criminal activity. Listen to your teacher, okay?"

It's not fair of you to only act like a teacher at a time like this, Naoya thought.

Nevertheless, Hana certainly couldn't tag along past this point. It was getting late, and they couldn't let her get mixed up in any danger.

Hana reluctantly agreed to go home after Takatsuki was able to mollify her by saying he would contact her after he was done looking into the house.

"Really, you have to, okay? You absolutely have to contact me. I don't want to hear that you've gone missing, too, okay?"

They escorted Hana, who anxiously repeated the same question over and over—to the bus stop. After she was gone, Takatsuki turned to Naoya once more.

"...Time for you to go home as well, Fukamachi."

"I don't want to."

Takatsuki looked troubled.

"Come on now, you've got to listen to your professor. If something happened to you, I really wouldn't be able to face your parents."

"My parents have nothing to do with this... They rarely want anything to do with me anyway."

"You shouldn't say that."

Takatsuki sighed, then looked slightly up toward the sky.

Naoya followed suit. The sky at the end of September got dark quickly, compared to how it had been in the height of summer. The sun was already sinking below the western horizon, leaving only a faint afterglow behind.

Standing in front of the well-lit train station, he couldn't quite make out the stars, but night was already starting to unfurl across the sky. The trailing clouds were turning indigo before the sky itself, which was still clinging to the faint light of day. Beneath the clouds, several ravens were flying by.

Following their flapping black silhouettes with his eyes, Naoya spoke.

"...There are birds living in that house."

Takatsuki looked at him in surprise.

With a slightly mean-spirited smile, Naoya turned his gaze to the professor.

"What are you going to do if you come across a bird inside?"

"...I'll make sure not to go upstairs, so it'll be fine. They generally only build their nests on upper floors. The first floor should be safe."

"But you can't be sure that's the case, right?"

Takatsuki's brow furrowed, and his mouth snapped shut.

Feeling a little buoyed by besting Takatsuki for the first time, Naoya leaned in close toward the other man all at once, using his own habit against him. He carried on talking, his face near Takatsuki's.

"Don't you think it's better if I go, too? Wouldn't you hate it if you encountered some birds in there and fainted, and then the birds landed on you and pecked at you and pooped on you?"

"…Don't say something like that; it's too disgusting to even imagine."

Takatsuki leaned back a little to get away from Naoya, a genuinely repulsed look on his face. Apparently, he couldn't take it as well as he could give it out. It was kind of funny.

For a while, Takatsuki glared up at the sky, looking grossed out. Then, as he lowered his chin again, he put a hand on top of Naoya's head. Even though there was already a height difference between them, out of nowhere, Takatsuki's hand pushed down hard on Naoya's head, forcing him even lower.

"Fukamachi, you're quite the cheeky little brat, aren't you?!"

"Hey, wh-what are you doing?!"

Takatsuki's hand ruffled Naoya's hair violently as Naoya flailed and struggled.

Somehow, Naoya managed to escape Takatsuki's hold, and when he turned back around, trying to tame his tousled hair, he found Takatsuki laughing.

"…I guess I have no choice, hmm? Fine, then. Let's go together. But in exchange, if something happens, you have to get out of there before me."

"What do you mean, 'something'?"

"I mean in case whatever is in that house is a criminal or a monster."

"You would include monsters on the list of possibilities, wouldn't you?"

"What's wrong with that?! Like I said, there's a nonzero possibility!"

With that retort, Takatsuki puffed up sullenly like a child.

* * *

After waiting for night to fall, Naoya and Takatsuki returned once more to the abandoned house.

In the dark, the house looked just like something out of a horror movie, and Naoya came to a stop in front of the gate. He swallowed reflexively. Perhaps hearing that sound, Takatsuki looked over at him, speaking in a quiet voice.

"If you're scared, it's okay to wait here, you know?"

"...I'm not scared."

Takatsuki gave a small snort of laughter at his reply. Annoyed, Naoya stepped ahead of the other man and approached the gate.

When he tried to push it open, the gate creaked. He reined in the pressure from his hand immediately. Ever so slowly, as quietly as possible, he eased open the gate.

As Naoya was about to step toward the front door, Takatsuki tapped him on the shoulder. He gestured toward the side entrance, which was accessible through the yard, and seemed to be indicating they should go in that way. They tramped through the overgrown grass into the yard. Autumn insects chirped away as they approached the building. Naoya had a mini flashlight at the ready, but he didn't dare turn it on yet. He didn't want to alert anyone in the area, and there was also the possibility that, if someone was inside the house, they would take notice.

The rain shutters on the first floor were pulled shut. Takatsuki stepped quietly up onto the porch and tried the first set of shutters. The first set didn't budge, but the next ones moved with a small squeak. Takatsuki looked over his shoulder at Naoya, who nodded back at him. Together, they pushed open the shutters at a silent, glacial pace.

Once there was a gap big enough for a person to go through, Takatsuki reached past the shutters to the interior glass door and pushed it. It slid open smoothly.

The professor crept in through the narrow opening, Naoya on his heels.

Inside, the room was Japanese style. By the light of the outdoor lamp that was streaming in, Naoya could just make out an old chest of drawers and a dressing table.

Takatsuki suddenly squatted down where he stood. Ignoring Naoya, who stood over him wondering what on earth he was doing, Takatsuki trailed his fingers over the straw tatami floor. He seemed to be checking the condition of the floor. Compared to how it looked on the outside, the house's interior wasn't very worn down. Nodding once, Takatsuki took off his leather shoes. Following suit, Naoya removed his sneakers.

Takatsuki pulled the glass door nearly closed, leaving a small gap. Moving quietly over the tatami floor, they stopped at the room's entrance and peered into the hallway.

It was quiet inside the house. There were no signs of activity. There certainly weren't any lights on, either.

Takatsuki took out his mini flashlight and continued down the corridor, examining the other rooms. There was a kitchen. Illuminated by the white light, the room really didn't feel that neglected. The calendar stuck to the wall was from two years prior. The cupboards and refrigerator were intact. Inexplicably, Naoya felt the urge to open the refrigerator. It didn't seem to be plugged in, but maybe there was something inside… Like a body.

Takatsuki tapped him on the shoulder again.

He looked to the corner of the room, where Takatsuki was pointing, and saw a bunch of convenience store bags scattered about. It looked like there were leftover food wrappers and plastic bottles inside the bags.

Someone had been here, after all.

Takatsuki went farther into the house. Beyond the kitchen was a living room with a sofa and television inside. A faint, strange smell hung in the air. It was a grassy, cloying smell Naoya had never encountered before.

Takatsuki's flashlight landed on a glass door that seemed to lead into the yard, and something odd caught Naoya's eye.

Instead of a curtain, the door was covered in brown packing tape, as if someone had tried to seal up the opening.

It made him think of people who died by suicide by burning charcoal in an enclosed space. Could someone have tried to do that in the house? But there weren't any dead bodies, and the smell wafting through the room didn't seem like burned charcoal.

Takatsuki picked up something from under the sofa and shone his light on it.

It was a withered, palm-shaped leaf.

"...I see," Takatsuki murmured softly. "So that's what's going on."

"Professor...? What is that?"

"It's cannabis. Someone was growing cannabis here."

Takatsuki's voice had gone dull.

Naoya stared in shock at the leaf in Takatsuki's hand. Wasn't cannabis used to make narcotics? Was it legal to grow something like that?

It couldn't be, if it was being done like this in a deserted old house.

"This is an unexpectedly boring outcome, isn't it?"

Takatsuki spoke.

"Some unsavory sort must have had their eye on this house once it was abandoned. They've been growing cannabis here in secret. It's probably necessary to control the amount of light used in growing cannabis, so they taped off the door to totally block outside light from coming in. That sort of thing."

He pointed his flashlight at the packing tape again.

"Whoever it is probably doesn't live here but comes by now and then to tend to the plants. They might even have spread the rumor that this house is haunted. Told it to children to keep them away, possibly... Although, it seems there are kids like Miss Sayuki who were drawn in by the story instead."

"Then Sayuki—"

"More than likely, the bad guys just happened to be here when she sneaked in, and they ran into each other. She wasn't fully conscious when she was found, right? They probably forced her to get high. Then they weren't sure what to do with her, loaded her into a car to avoid being seen, and dumped her in Hachiōji."

"But cannabis... Couldn't they find something like that in someone's system right away with a drug test?"

"If this was America, sure. But here, when a missing minor is found, administering a drug test isn't usually the first thing on anyone's mind. Miss Sayuki was lucky not to be killed."

Takatsuki's words were terrifying.

But that could very well have happened, couldn't it? Because the beings haunting this house weren't monsters—they were criminals.

"So what do we do?"

"Hmm, I'm guessing they moved their growing operation somewhere else after the incident with Miss Sayuki. If so, it would be hard to track them down. But we can't pretend we didn't see it, either. For now, let's consult KenKen."

Takatsuki took a picture of the leaf he was holding with his phone. He emailed the photo to Sasakura, along with the house's GPS information.

The response was immediate.

"...Ah. He's mad. He says, 'What are you doing, stupid?'"

Takatsuki smiled wryly at the message on his phone.

"He says he's on his way. Let's go outside for the time be—"

Something interrupted him.

The sound of a car outside.

With a start, Takatsuki turned off his flashlight. They heard what sounded like the slamming of a car door, right outside the house. It couldn't be.

They both headed for the Japanese-style room they had first entered, but Takatsuki was quicker. He moved easily through the dark without bumping into anything. He might have memorized the house's layout and the location of the furniture as they came inside.

By the time Naoya, who had to fumble and stagger his way forward, made it to the room, Takatsuki was peering outside through the crack he had left in the door. He quickly picked up both his and Naoya's shoes and moved away from the door. Takatsuki met Naoya's gaze and shook his head slightly. Someone was making their way into the house. Someone—well, it had to be the people who had grown the cannabis. Naoya looked at the professor with a pleading gaze. Takatsuki's keen eyes surveyed their surroundings, then he grabbed Naoya's arm and pulled him into the hallway. They found the staircase, climbed up a few steps, and hunkered down. Apparently, the plan was to hide behind the staircase wall and wait until the danger was past.

As soon as they squatted down, Naoya heard the rain shutters moving. The shutters were pulled open with a clatter, much more carelessly than Naoya and Takatsuki had done. Naoya supposed if the criminals were going in and out of the house often, they were probably used to the sound. Then there was the creaking of the tatami floor. They were inside the house.

They were having a conversation loudly enough to be overheard.

"...Hey, are you serious about that? Settin' a fire. Didn't we get rid of pretty much anything incriminating? There's nothing left that could be used as evidence. I don't think we gotta go that far."

"I'm not takin' any chances. We don't know if that girl is gonna squeal about this place... We did make her smoke a whole bunch, though, so she coulda forgot."

The voices belonged to two men. They were still in the Japanese-style room.

But the topic of conversation was horrifying. "Setting a fire." Did that mean they were planning to burn the whole house down to destroy the evidence?

Takatsuki looked back at Naoya and pressed his index finger to his lips. *Keep quiet*, he was saying. Phone in hand, he fired off another email to Sasakura.

After a while spent waiting on the stairs, the two men moved from the Japanese-style room to the living room. The sound of footsteps walking about was followed by the creak of the sofa springs. Apparently, they were sitting down.

Very quietly, Takatsuki put on his shoes. Naoya slipped into his sneakers just as carefully.

The front door was right across from the stairs. It was the fastest route out. Takatsuki and Naoya locked eyes, nodded, and slowly crept down the stairs. Naoya stepped down into the foyer, and—

Clang!

There was a metallic crash at Naoya's feet.

Crap, Naoya thought, face crumpling into a grimace. It felt like he had kicked an empty metal bucket or something.

"Hey! Who's there?!"

A man's voice shouted from the living room. Spotting the two of them, the man started sprinting in their direction.

"Fukamachi, the door!"

Takatsuki pushed Naoya toward the front door, then turned back and stepped into the hallway. He was protecting Naoya.

Naoya turned the doorknob, but the door didn't open. For an instant, he almost panicked, then realized it must be locked and hurriedly slid back the bolt. As he struggled with the door, he could hear the man who had run toward them taking a swing at Takatsuki. When he heard something hit the wall with a *bang,* he reflexively looked over his shoulder to find Takatsuki pinning the other man up against the hallway.

"Fukamachi, hurry!" the professor yelled.

Naoya turned the knob again, and this time, it opened. *Yes,* he thought, pushing on the door—but it only opened a few inches before stopping short with a clatter. Eyes wide in fear, Naoya tried to find out why—and saw it. The door chain was fastened. Berating himself for his stupidity, he tried to remove it. It wouldn't budge. His panicked fingers fumbled with the chain, but that wasn't the problem. It was rusted in place.

"Fukamachi!"

"It's no use; it won't open!"

On the verge of tears, Naoya yelled back and heard Takatsuki click his tongue. By that time, the other criminal had descended upon them. Holding the first man against the wall with one hand, Takatsuki used his free arm to guard himself from the second man's raised fist. He swept the first man's legs out from underneath him with his foot, sending the man crashing to the floor. But in the time it took him to do that, the second man, who looked stronger than the first, had seized Takatsuki by the collar.

He slammed Takatsuki into the wall with brute force.

The man sunk several punches into Takatsuki's stomach, and the professor's knees buckled.

"...!"

Shouting incoherently, Naoya launched himself into the fray. Deliberately treading on the first man, who was trying to get up from the floor, he threw himself headfirst into the flank of the man who was holding Takatsuki against the wall. Caught off guard, the man lost his balance, and Takatsuki pushed himself away from the wall. He punched the second man in the face, then grabbed Naoya's arm and shoved him up the stairs without a word. There was only one way out now.

Naoya ran toward the second floor with Takatsuki behind him. The angry bellows of the two criminals followed him as well. He was too afraid to look over his shoulder. As he set foot on the second floor, the men's voices suddenly shifted from furious yells to shouts of surprise, accompanied by the sound of something tumbling down the stairs. Glancing back instinctively, he saw Takatsuki with one foot aloft. He seemed to have kicked their pursuers back down to the first floor.

"Professor!"

"Just get to the back room!"

Naoya rushed into the rearmost room at Takatsuki's chastising tone. Takatsuki followed him in, and Naoya could see the two men dashing up the stairs after them once more. Heart in his throat, Naoya slammed the room's sliding door shut. He noticed Takatsuki heaving a bookcase over from next to the door and jumped in to help. Just before the men reached them, they shoved the bookcase up against the door, pinning it in place. The men pounded on the door, but Naoya and Takatsuki threw their body weight against the shelf to keep the door jammed shut.

"Fukamachi, go see whether we can get out through the window—"
Takatsuki broke off midsentence as a rustling noise resounded in the
room, mixing with his voice.

Startled, Takatsuki's whole body started to tremble.

Despairingly, Naoya turned to look around the room.

Countless flashes of white crossed his field of vision.

Feathers.

He heard Takatsuki suck in a breath.

Neither of them, when they were rushing to get into the room, had
noticed the state of things beyond the door.

This was the room with the broken window. A group of pigeons
perched on the shelves across from the window. It looked like they were
nesting there. The commotion must have agitated them, because all at
once, the birds started flapping their wings. Dozens of pigeons were flying around the room.

Takatsuki crumpled to his knees.

"Professor!"

Clutching his head in both hands, Takatsuki groaned. He was shaking from head to toe. With him down, it became a lot harder to hold the
door shut. Naoya pressed his back into the bookcase, leaning his whole
weight against it, and shouted at Takatsuki.

"Professor! Professor, please pull it together!"

"...Stop... No..."

Curled into a ball on the floor, Takatsuki started to scream.

"Professor! Professor Takatsuki!"

"No, stop...! Let me go, no...!"

"Professor! Professor!"

Naoya called out desperately to the other man as nonsensical mutter-
ings fell from his mouth.

Then, suddenly, Takatsuki raised his head.

Naoya stared in shock. The professor's wide-open eyes were glowing
blue.

The birds were still flying around the room. The outside light streaming in through the torn shoji screen illuminated the birds' white feathers as they floated to the floor and shone on Takatsuki, hunched beneath them.

But the light coming from Takatsuki's eyes was shining brighter.

"No... Stop, I'm begging you..."

His glowing blue gaze was overflowing with terror.

"I... I don't...want to go..."

All at once, Takatsuki slumped forward onto the floor, like a puppet with its strings cut. Naoya immediately tried to reach for him but felt the door rattling behind him like it was about to slide open. Panicked, he pushed his weight back onto the bookshelf. He held the door closed, fighting back tears the whole time.

He wasn't sure how long that lasted. After what felt like an eternity, he suddenly realized that, at some point without his realizing it, the other side of the door had gone silent. He couldn't hear any angry voices or pounding.

Quietly, Naoya stood up and backed away from the bookshelf. He listened again for any noises from outside the room but didn't hear anything. Had the men left?

Naoya approached Takatsuki's fallen form and shook his shoulder. There was no reaction. He was out cold. He didn't so much as stir, even when Naoya whispered his name.

Then a strange smell filled Naoya's nose.

It was different from the one in the living room. It smelled burnt.

Alarmed, Naoya looked around for the source and noticed white smoke billowing in through a gap in the door.

What had those men been talking about when they entered the house earlier? Right— Something about setting a fire. Had they really done it? Were they actually planning to erase all the evidence in the house—and Naoya and Takatsuki along with it?

Hurriedly shoving the bookcase out of the way, he tugged on the door. It didn't move. Some kind of rod or something was jamming it shut from outside. Naoya banged on the door in desperation. This couldn't be real.

He went to the window and looked down, seeing smoke rising from below. It seemed like the only thing currently burning was the living room, but he knew the fire would eventually spread. This was bad.

"Professor! Please wake up! If we don't get out, we're going to burn to death!"

He tried waking Takatsuki, but it was useless. He would have to carry the unconscious man out. But no matter how hard he tried, Naoya was only strong enough to drag Takatsuki up for a minute. Sudden bursts of strength in emergencies—those kinds of things weren't real. There was no way he would be able to hoist him over his shoulder.

In the meantime, smoke continued to fill the room. He was starting to feel the heat from the flames, too. Coughs erupted from his lungs. Pulling Takatsuki's head into his own lap, Naoya looked down at the professor's face and silently begged him to wake up. But Takatsuki's long-lashed eyelids didn't even flutter.

What should he do? What could he do? How could things have come to this?

He never thought he could be this helpless. Looking between the smoke pouring into the room and the unconscious Takatsuki, Naoya felt utterly lost. He prayed to no one in particular for help. *Please come quickly. Someone. Anyone.* He took his smartphone from his pocket with trembling fingers. But who should he call? The fire department? The police? Would they even be able to make it in time?

The most reliable person Naoya knew, no matter what he usually said, was here, unconscious.

The smoke was getting worse. Taking out his handkerchief, Naoya covered Takatsuki's mouth. He pressed his own mouth to the top of his shoulder, trying to protect himself from breathing in the smoke, if only a little. Even if a neighbor noticed the fire and called for help, would he and Takatsuki be able to survive until help arrived? If he was supposed to be the Sensible One, why hadn't he stopped Takatsuki from coming here in the first place?

The professor was still unconscious.

"Professor...I absolutely do not want to die with you in a place like this..."

Takatsuki had told him to escape on his own if anything happened. As if he could do that.

Then—

Hearing the sound of a car coming to a stop in front of the house, Naoya's head snapped up.

"Akira! Fukamachi! Hey, where are you?!"

Sasakura's voice. He came for them.

Naoya screamed toward the window.

"Mr. Sasakura! We're on the second floor! The back room!"

There was no reply.

But moments later, he heard footsteps pounding up the stairs. "Back here!" Naoya tried to yell, coughing, right before a clanging sound came from outside the room.

Ripping the door open, Sasakura stepped inside.

"Akira! Fukamachi! Are you all right?!"

Feeling like he was about to sob with relief at the sight of Sasakura's huge, reliable form, Naoya somehow managed to say, "We're safe."

Although Naoya had struggled to even lift him, Sasakura hoisted Takatsuki onto his back with ease and carried him outside. The fire was spreading from the living room into the hallway, but it had only barely made it to the Japanese-style room that led into the yard.

As they stepped outside, a fire engine and a police car were just pulling up to the house. Sasakura carelessly tossed Takatsuki into the back seat of the car he was driving, pushed Naoya into the passenger seat, and had a short conversation with the uniformed police officer who got out of the patrol car.

Before long, he came back to the car he had put them in and climbed into the driver's seat.

"…I'm gonna take Akira home first."

A moment later, he turned the key in the ignition. Behind them, the firefighters had started battling the fire. For a little while, Naoya watched through the rear window as they blasted the blazing house with a fire hose. Then he turned his gaze to Takatsuki in the back seat.

The other man was sprawled listlessly across the seat, having not moved at all from how Sasakura had tossed him into the car.

"…"

As soon as Naoya opened his mouth, he started to cough. Sasakura, one hand on the wheel, held out a plastic bottle of water to him. It was open and partially consumed, but Naoya took it gratefully. The cool water seemed to seep into his smoke-parched throat.

"…U-um."

Sasakura shot a scowl at him when he opened his mouth again.

Naoya continued, even though that sharp glare momentarily tripped him up.

"Y-you came quickly."

"Yeah. I jumped in a car as soon as Akira emailed me."

Sasakura's voice was even huskier than usual, probably because of the smoke, and sounded like it would work well at intimidating someone.

"Is it okay that you left work? Won't the police department mind?"

"It was right at the end of my workday. I had to commandeer a car from a colleague, but it's probably fine."

Was it fine? Naoya didn't know.

The car looked like a regular vehicle from the outside, but it was actually an unmarked cop car. The incessantly chattering police radio was grating. Sasakura continued driving in silence. He was an unexpectedly careful driver. He only glanced away from the road for a second when the words "suspicious vehicle found" came over the radio.

After they had been on the road for a bit, Sasakura said, "Hey. Tell me what happened. It's gonna be a little while longer until we reach Akira's apartment."

Naoya told him everything that had gone on until that point.

When he mentioned *kamikakushi*, he thought he saw Sasakura's grip on the steering wheel twitch for a second, but other than that, he let Naoya keep talking without showing any signs of paying attention. At the end of the story, Sasakura let out a heavy sigh.

"...Dammit, you idiot!"

And slammed his fist into the side window with a *thud*.

Naoya apologized reflexively.

"I-I'm sorry, I'm really sorry."

"No, I'm not talking to you. I'm talking to the idiot passed out in the back, that dumbass!"

Sasakura snapped at him, looking even more like a rabid dog than usual.

Then he drummed his fingers against the steering wheel for a while, agitated, and sighed again.

"...For the time being, I'm gonna let the whole trespassing thing go."

"Um, do things like this happen a lot?" Naoya asked.

Sasakura scowled at him again.

"Yes."

He went back to drumming on the steering wheel.

He didn't know if that yes was in response to things like covering up the trespassing, Takatsuki losing consciousness and collapsing, or getting caught up in criminal activity. He didn't dare ask. He had a feeling the answer was all of the above anyway.

Takatsuki's apartment was in Yoyogi.

Sasakura heaved the still-unconscious Takatsuki onto his back again. Naoya searched Takatsuki's pockets to find the key, and once the door was open, he walked inside like he was thoroughly familiar with the place.

The two-bedroom apartment was meticulously clean. But just like Takatsuki's office, it was full of bookshelves. Unlike the shelves at the office, these ones were full of books that didn't have to do with the professor's research. There were collections of landscape photography and novels, among other things. Naoya even saw the spine of a book that he had read himself, and for some reason, he was both happy and a little surprised.

"...You have this many books at home, Professor?"

"What?"

Hearing Naoya muttering to himself, Sasakura turned around.

"No, it's just—he can memorize every sentence and picture simply from reading something once, right? So I thought he wouldn't have any books at home."

"Ah. He says he enjoys his favorite books no matter how many times he's read them. I tried to tell him once he should throw some out because this place was overflowing with books. Said it was fine since he'd remember them anyway. He told me, 'Just as someone can be happy no matter how many times they see someone they love, reading a favorite book is enjoyable no matter how many times you reread it...' I don't really get it, but whatever."

Sasakura snorted. Apparently, he wasn't a big reader.

"Anyway, bring me some towels from that bathroom over there. I'm gonna put this guy to bed for now, but if I lay him down before he gets cleaned up, he'll get mad at me later for the sheets getting dirty. He's really annoying like that."

Following Sasakura's instructions, Naoya spread the bathroom towels over the bed and pillows. After removing Takatsuki's jacket, Sasakura laid him on the bed. Hair disheveled and face streaked with soot, Takatsuki was a mere shadow of his usually gentlemanly self.

Trying to at least clean up his face, Naoya wiped at the ash with a damp towel. Even then, the professor showed no signs of stirring.

Understandably concerned, Naoya turned to Sasakura.

"Um. Is he really okay? He's not waking up at all."

"It's like tripping a circuit breaker. He'll recover if we just leave him be."

"...He's not a laptop."

"It's similar, okay? Anyway, he's not gonna be waking up for a while, so if you wanna draw on his face or something, there's a pen over there."

You could give him nose hairs, write *idiot* on his forehead, whatever you want."

"I-I'm not going to do that...! I mean, he got beat up by those guys earlier. I'm worried about that, too."

"Beat up? Where?"

"His stomach, I'm pretty sure... He got hit a few times..."

Hearing that, Sasakura frowned and looked down at Takatsuki.

"...Well, it doesn't look like he's vomited at all. He's probably fine, but...I might as well check to be safe."

He started unbuttoning Takatsuki's shirt. With his torso bared, Naoya could see several spots around his stomach that had turned red. They must have been where he was punched.

Sasakura put his hand to the area gently.

"No fever, either. I'm pretty sure he'll be all right like this."

He started to button Takatsuki's shirt back up, then seemed to decide it was too troublesome halfway through.

"He's gonna change when he wakes up anyway. I guess there's no need to button it."

Muttering that to himself, Sasakura roughly yanked a discarded futon up over Takatsuki. Naoya wasn't sure if his generally careless treatment of the other man was because they were longtime friends or if it was just a matter of personality.

Takatsuki's upper half was still mostly uncovered due to the sloppy way the futon had been put over him. He shouldn't be cold at this time of year, but Naoya fixed the futon anyway. His bare skin was quite pale, compared to most men, and it made the red spots where he had been hit stand out even more pitifully.

As he adjusted the futon, Naoya suddenly remembered what Ruiko had told him.

There were two scars on Takatsuki's back that looked like someone had cut off his wings, she had said.

The professor was totally passed out. If Naoya turned him over now, would he be able to see those scars?

"Hey. What're you doing?"

Sasakura's voice took him by surprise. Unconsciously, Naoya had reached a hand toward Takatsuki's shoulder.

He withdrew his hand in a flash and looked over at Sasakura.

"U-um."

He started to say something, but Sasakura's razor-sharp gaze stopped him, and he dropped his eyes back to Takatsuki.

Asleep, he looked just like a finely crafted doll. With his face placid, it was easy to see how well-formed his features were.

Naoya felt like he was looking down at an unfamiliar face, probably because the Takatsuki in his mind was always smiling.

"Um."

He remembered.

Takatsuki's eyes, right before he collapsed.

His glowing blue gaze, the color of the night sky.

"No, I don't want to go," he had said. Something like that.

Like he was seeing something from the past.

"Um, Mr. Sasakura... Can I ask you something?"

"What is it?"

"What on earth happened to Professor Takatsuki?"

The question slipped from Naoya's mouth.

Sasakura raised one eyebrow.

"What on earth happened to make him like this?"

There was something else, too. One other recollection.

In Takatsuki's office, right before the end of summer break.

The odd thing Takatsuki had said to him after Naoya told him everything about what happened when he was young.

"If someone is disgusted by you, I'm sure they would be disgusted by me as well, you know."

He had been trying to deduce the meaning behind those words ever since.

It was as if Takatsuki was saying he and Naoya were one and the same.

Eyes the color of the night sky. An extraordinarily strong memory.

The more he thought about it, the less those traits seemed like normal human features.

The same way that Naoya's ears weren't normal.

Was Takatsuki also…?

"…Why do you want to know?"

Sasakura's rebuttal was the same as it had been when Naoya asked before.

"I'm not sure. But…it's not just out of curiosity. Really, genuinely…I want to know."

Even if it meant crossing a line.

After all, Takatsuki had already stepped over the lines Naoya had drawn when Naoya told him everything.

So Naoya wanted to know about Takatsuki, even if it meant reaching out over the barriers surrounding him.

He wanted to know the real shape of this man who was always smiling.

Sasakura looked down at Naoya and clicked his tongue.

Then he turned on his heel and started to leave the room, and Naoya hurriedly called out after him.

"M-Mr. Sasakura—"

"Come with me. Akira will be fine here. Let's get something to drink."

Sasakura shepherded Naoya onto the couch in the living room, then went to the kitchen.

Unabashedly, like he really was used to doing so, he started rooting around in the refrigerator.

"Dammit, no actual food in here, as usual… He doesn't really cook, you see… Thinks he's funny, putting shit like mozzarella cheese in here… Well, it's still good, so we might as well eat it."

Sasakura muttered threateningly to himself and pulled out a ball of cheese and a tomato.

After a little while, he came back with a plate of sliced mozzarella and tomato drizzled with olive oil. Considering Takatsuki didn't cook often, Naoya was surprised to see he at least had some things that could be served as snacks. Somehow that felt befitting of an adult man. Especially for one who usually only ate sweets.

Sasakura also grabbed a bottle of wine from a shelf. He started to pour two glasses, then paused.

"...Fukamachi. Are you still underage?"

"Yes."

"No wine for you, then. I'm pretty sure there was some ginger ale in the fridge; have some of that."

He jutted his chin toward the refrigerator. Go get it yourself, he seemed to be saying. He was a police officer, Naoya remembered. He probably didn't approve of underage drinking.

Peeking into the refrigerator, Naoya saw a bottle of dry ginger ale. He didn't like drinking sweet things, but he thought he could handle this, so he grabbed the bottle and went back to the couch.

Sasakura was already sipping at his wine when he started to speak.

"Akira was spirited away when he was twelve."

"Huh...?"

Naoya's eyes widened. Without thinking, he glanced over at the bedroom.

"He disappeared one night from the second floor of his house in Setagaya. His parents were in the living room on the first floor, and there were no signs of anyone leaving through the front door. None of his shoes were gone, and there was nothing in particular taken from his room. Only the window in his room was open. Him running away seemed too improbable, but as a kidnapping, it was weird, too. When they hadn't found him after a week, it became an open criminal investigation. But he still didn't turn up. The media labeled it *kamikakushi* because the circumstances were so strange."

Sasakura took a break from talking to gulp down his wine. Drinking the bloodred liquid like water, he drained his glass and poured another one.

"The police suspected kidnapping, but there was never any demand for ransom or anything. His mother was frantic; his father was run ragged. Then, after a month—they found him."

He turned up in Kyoto, over five hours away. He was found lying unconscious in the road near Kurama, as if someone had just discarded him.

"He wasn't wearing shoes when they found him, but the soles of his feet were clean. So the police thought someone had transported him in a car and abandoned him there. Although, they didn't get any leads on a suspicious vehicle or anything."

I've heard this story before, Naoya thought. It was a lot like Sayuki's story. And—it was very similar to the story Takatsuki had told in his class, about the young man who had been moved from Kyoto to Asakusa. The story of Yasujirou, the man who was kidnapped by *tengu.*

"There was one more thing. When they found him, Akira was bleeding from his back. Two huge strips of skin were missing. Like someone carved two long, narrow triangles from his shoulder blades down to his hip bones."

Details of his injuries were kept from the media. But laying eyes on those wounds had been a huge shock for his family. Their young son was scarred for life.

"When he regained consciousness, he couldn't remember anything from the time he was gone. But he was different after that. He was petrified of birds, and his memory improved massively... And the color of his eyes, sometimes it would change."

In the end, the police couldn't find a single clue regarding what happened to Takatsuki.

Of course, his family was happy to have their son returned to them safely. But not knowing what had happened to their son in the month he was missing seemed to wear on them greatly. People feared what they could not explain. On top of that, the son they got back was a little different than the one they had lost. They had no idea why his eyes would occasionally turn indigo, why his memory was so strong, why he would break down and faint when he saw a bird.

"He had one relative who was a little strange. One day, that old hag said to Akira's mother, 'I'm certain Akira was carried away by the Kurama *tengu*. When he was about to become a *tengu*, they cut off his wings and returned him to the human world.'"

"...Now that you mention it, Professor Takatsuki did say in class before that Kurama had a long history of *tengu* folklore."

Ordinarily, his mother probably would have dismissed those words as utter drivel.

But at the time, she couldn't understand her son's changes, and she was mentally fatigued.

She ended up believing it. Her own son was almost turned into a *tengu*.

Tengu had wings. His fear of birds, the marks on his back—they were proof that he had almost become something inhuman.

"Then, well... A lot happened, and he didn't want to be at home anymore. He went to live with relatives overseas for a few years, then came back to Japan before university and started living on his own. Akira's parents are rich, so they supported him quite a bit financially... Only financially, though."

Sasakura practically spat out the details of Takatsuki's circumstances at the time.

It reminded Naoya of his own parents, whose faces went hopelessly stiff whenever they looked at him, after the incident.

Had Takatsuki's parents looked at him that way, too? Or maybe they had just stopped looking at him altogether.

...Had they told him that he creeped them out?

Takatsuki was always smiling. Smiling and amiable.

Naoya had thought, surely, he was someone who had grown up receiving love from those around him. He thought that was why Takatsuki was able to smile that brightly—and was kind to anyone and everyone.

He had no idea what Takatsuki had been hiding behind that sunny face.

Naoya had squeezed the bottle of ginger ale in his hands as he listened to Sasakura talk.

He wished that Sasakura's voice would warp.

It was the first time he had ever wished for that. For something to be a lie. Even an exaggeration would be fine. As long as what Sasakura was saying wasn't true.

But the other man's voice was mercilessly clear, and Naoya felt hopelessly saddened by it.

Sasakura drained his glass before speaking again.

"I don't really care what happened to him while he was gone. He came back; that's what matters. Whether he was turned into a *tengu* or abducted by aliens and experimented on, it's irrelevant to me. But I guess his so-called family didn't think that way. When he came back from abroad, Akira could have studied law or economics or medicine—whatever he liked. He was certainly smart enough. But he said he wanted to study folklore. He went from college to graduate school, and in no time, he became an associate professor. I think the reason he only wants to study urban legends and ghost stories and stuff like that is because he himself thinks what happened to him might be supernatural somehow. Although, I don't especially think that it is. Basically every case, just like this one, has ended up turning out nothing but criminals. It's dangerous. This isn't the first time Akira's gotten mixed up in a crime. But what scares me more…is the possibility that, someday, he'll encounter something real."

Sasakura continued.

"Crime is fine. I'm an officer, so I can do something about that. But if the monsters are real, I won't be able to help."

"…I suppose the police don't get involved in such cases."

"It's not like we're totally uninvolved… Just, it's a different jurisdiction."

"Jurisdiction? Is there a department that specializes in supernatural cases?"

"It's not public knowledge, but yeah. The person who runs it is someone I really don't want to be indebted to, though, so I don't fraternize with 'em."

Sasakura frowned hard. He didn't really get it, but Naoya thought whoever it was must be a bother. There was no way someone who was involved in those kinds of cases wouldn't be troublesome.

Naoya took a sip of the ginger ale—he had forgotten to drink it when he was squeezing the bottle tight—and found it had already gotten lukewarm. Maybe because of the temperature, it seemed like it was sweeter than before.

"Um."

"What is it?"

"…Would it be okay if I had some wine?"

"Of course it wouldn't; you're underage… More importantly—"

Suddenly, Sasakura tapped Naoya gently on the head.

"Hey, what are you doing? Is this police brutality?"

"Shut up, brat… If you were gonna cry, you shouldn't have said you wanted to hear the story, dummy."

He rapped Naoya's head again.

"I'm not crying," Naoya replied, sniffling.

The next day, the news was already reporting about the incident at the abandoned house. The fleeing criminals were apprehended that very night, having been caught in a trap set by the police. The fact that they had been cultivating cannabis had already gotten out. The perpetrators apparently said they had been growing it "for their own personal use."

Takatsuki and Naoya weren't mentioned in the news reports at all. Thankfully, neither was Sayuki's case. It was better to avoid having something she couldn't even remember being involved in being made into a circus by the media. It would just cause more damage.

A few days after the event, Naoya paid a visit to Takatsuki's office.

When he walked in, Takatsuki looked over his shoulder and smiled softly, as if nothing had changed.

"Hi there, Fukamachi... I'm sorry about the other night. Putting you in danger like that."

Naoya couldn't think of what to say in response to Takatsuki's terribly apologetic expression, so he muttered ineffective platitudes like "It's fine" and "I don't mind."

That day, Naoya had left Takatsuki's apartment before the professor had woken up. He hadn't known when Takatsuki would regain consciousness or how he should face him once he did.

Seeing Naoya's present demeanor, Takatsuki looked embarrassed.

"...I see. KenKen told you, didn't he? About me."

Apparently Sasakura hadn't told Takatsuki that Naoya knew. Surmising the answer from Naoya's behavior alone, Takatsuki smiled wryly.

He gestured toward a chair, and Naoya sat in it as directed. As always, Takatsuki went to make them drinks. Sugary cocoa for himself, bitter coffee for Naoya.

Naoya watched his back as he made the drinks.

Then he asked, "Is the reason you study urban legends and ghost stories that you're looking for cases like your own?"

Takatsuki froze.

Naoya looked at his unmoving form and kept talking.

"Is that why you collect strange stories? Because you want to find out what happened to you back then?"

"...Not knowing is scary."

Takatsuki turned around.

Drinks in hand, he walked over to Naoya and held out the Great Buddha cup, saying, "Here you go." He brought his own blue mug to his mouth, took a sip, and smiled. The scents of cocoa and coffee were mixing in the office air, slowly melting into the predominant smell of old books.

"I don't know if I was carried off by *tengu*, because I don't remember anything. It's possible I was actually just kidnapped by a common pervert who injected me with some weird drug to change my eye color and the contents of my mind, used me as a plaything, and after a while, peeled the skin off my back... If that's the case, it's possible that skin is somewhere out there still. After all, if it were me, I would definitely keep it safe."

Takatsuki's eyes were half closed and vacant, as if he was enjoying the smell of his cocoa. His pink tongue trailed quickly over the rim of the mug, and he smiled.

It was a dreadful, spine-chilling smile.

"If that really is the case—if the skin from my back is being preserved by someone somewhere, I have no intention of ever letting that person get away with it. Someone keeping the skin they cut off my back—just imagining it makes my skin crawl."

Takatsuki said so with a smile and took another sip of cocoa.

"Looking at what happened to me from one angle, I was spirited away. From a different angle, I was the victim of a crime... There are so many ghost stories and other tales in the world that are like that. You've already seen it, haven't you? After spending time with me."

That was true. An apartment that might be haunted, girls cursed by needles, *kamikakushi*. All of it had been done by humans.

Takatsuki put down his cup with a *clunk*, then propped up his chin with one hand. His currently dark-brown eyes were looking off into space. Naoya couldn't tell what those eyes were seeing. It could have been a memory of the past, or he could have been looking at the spine of the book that was in his line of sight.

"Often, behind the birth of strange stories, there are real-life incidents that are too gruesome to tell. People find comfort in adapting those unsavory incidents into legends and fables."

Things that were too painful in reality were bearable in fiction.

They could even be enjoyed, if people thought of them as nothing more than stories with no bearing on their actual circumstances.

That's why the world was full of legends and fairy tales.

Most people never turned their attention to the truth that was being concealed behind the story.

But—

"Folklore studies is a discipline in which the background of the birth of those legends and fables is investigated and researched. In other words, the field's purpose is to find out the true events hidden in the fairy tales. That being the case, if I can solve cases like my own, I might be able to figure out what happened to me. And that means…I might be able to do the same for you."

Takatsuki continued.

"My eyes, the scars on my back—your ears, too. We probably won't be able to go back to how we were. At this point, even if we find the causes, nothing may change. That's what Kenji says, at least. He's told me so before, you know. But I think…knowing is better than not knowing. I would rather tear my eyes out than ignore the truth just to live."

Head still cradled in his hand, Takatsuki's gaze suddenly lit on Naoya.

"What about you, Fukamachi?"

"Me?"

"Don't you want to know what really happened to you that night when you were ten?"

The truth of that festival of the dead.

Every year for four years after that, until his grandmother passed away, Naoya went to her house. But he was never able to go to that midnight festival again, and neither his grandmother nor his relatives could tell him anything about it when he asked. He suspected his grandmother probably knew something, but when questioned, she only replied, "It's better if you don't know," and refused to say more.

Naoya had thought he would never learn the truth.

But maybe…

Maybe with this person—with Takatsuki—they could figure it out.

"In order to learn everything I can, I'm going to continue my research. And if possible, I would like you to help me with it. I won't force you. You already know it can be dangerous. Just look at what happened the other day. But…I would be happy if you were here. Perhaps there are things that we, as people who may have actually experienced the supernatural, will be able to understand."

Ah, Naoya thought.

Maybe what Ruiko had said was right.

Maybe Takatsuki was a fallen angel.

Because the invitation to join him was like being tempted by the devil. Telling Naoya, who thought he would be alone forever, that there was someone just like him right here?

How could he resist that?

Naoya put his cup on the table.

He glanced at the multicolored Great Buddha, then looked back at Takatsuki.

"Um. I think I'll bring my own cup next time, if that's okay."

"Huh?"

"I want to try drinking this coffee in a cup that doesn't have the Great Buddha on it."

Takatsuki took his elbow off the table. He leaned slightly toward Naoya, staring intently at his face.

Huh, Naoya thought, seeing that expression, *he was more anxious than I expected*. Even though he had acted all cool when he said he wouldn't force it.

"I...want to know, too. About what happened to me—and to you. All of it."

"...F-Fukamachi!"

Takatsuki's eyes lit up. *Ah, there it is*. That golden retriever smile. An affable, friendly smile that seemed to say, "I'm so happy I can barely stand it."

"Then, Fukamachi... Um, well, I look forward to working with you more in the future!"

Takatsuki stuck out his right hand. Naoya wondered if the habit of invading people's personal space and immediately asking for a handshake was one he picked up while living abroad.

It wasn't really customary in Japan to shake hands, he thought, taking Takatsuki's hand with his own anyway.

"Yes… Thank you very much."

Naoya contemplated which cup he should bring in as his personal one. In the end, he decided to go with one he had at home. He had bought it ages ago, because it had a picture of a dog on it. A dog that reminded him of Leo, his old golden retriever.